NOW
IS THE TIME

Also by Lillian Smith

THE JOURNEY

KILLERS OF THE DREAM

STRANGE FRUIT

NOW IS THE TIME
by Lillian Smith

New York

THE VIKING PRESS

1955

To Children Everywhere

```
E          Smith, Lillian Eugenia
185.61
.S646      Now is the time.

379 S5
```

COPYRIGHT 1955 BY LILLIAN SMITH

PUBLISHED BY THE VIKING PRESS IN FEBRUARY 1955

PUBLISHED ON THE SAME DAY IN THE DOMINION OF CANADA
BY THE MACMILLAN COMPANY OF CANADA LIMITED

Library of Congress catalog card number: 55-6717

PRINTED IN U. S. A. BY THE COLONIAL PRESS, INC.

Contents

I: Now Is the Time   9

II: There Are Things to Do and Things to Say   75

III: The Twenty-five Questions   97

Books You May Want to Read   121

NOW
IS THE TIME

I

Now Is the Time

❖ 1 ❖

IT WAS May seventeenth. Many of us sat at radio and television, waiting. For word had gone out that the Supreme Court would hand down its decision on segregation in the public schools, that day.

Events at home and abroad had confused and shocked us: the Army-McCarthy hearings, evasion and postponement in Congress, headline squabbles, suspicion of good men, trials, more and more investigations—and all the while, the Communist powers were moving like a tidal wave across Asia, dividing and weakening each country they touched.

China, years ago, had been lost to the free world. Korea had been divided. Now we were watching it happen in Indochina. It too would be lost or divided. The next? And next?

A feeling was creeping from person to person, group to group, a clear sense: that things need not be like this. Why was communism winning Asia? Why was this new tyranny so seductive that the people ran out and grasped it?

Until two centuries ago, the idea of freedom was only a dream; the human being's importance was only an ideal. Tyranny and slavery were the realities of man's experience. Then, suddenly, the dream, the ideal, grew into a bold and beautiful political system called democracy. Men said that never, hereafter, would human beings be satisfied with anything less. When they heard of it they would demand it as their right.

Now, here were a billion people craving this new freedom, thinking of human dignity, hungering for it—and millions of them settling for new and heavier chains of bondage.

Why? We knew why even as we asked. We knew democracy had not met their needs. Somehow, the dream had walled itself off. Somehow it had become segregated. In the eyes of Asia and Africa democracy had turned into "white democracy." They do not trust the white hands that offer them aid because, until now, those hands have given them only the bitter experiences of colonialism and white prestige. They are reluctant to accept the United States as a friend—this democracy which has never colonized any Asian or African country —because its people cling to color segregation and have laws in many states making it compulsory.

Why don't we see this? People were asking—more and more of them.

And so we waited that day, tense and expectant.

We knew what the decision would be. The necessities of our times had clearly determined it: not alone the world situation but the human situation here at home, in our children's lives, in our own hearts and minds, made it imperative that the highest authority in our land say clearly that there is no place, today, for legal segregation in a free and democratic nation. We knew. But we wanted to hear it said aloud. And when the words came, simple and plain, a deep pride swept across America.

Chief Justice Warren, who spoke for a unanimous court, did not clutter his pages with legal precedents. He based the decision on a truth more important than precedents: a child's right to learn. He stated, for the first time in the history of a country's highest court, that a child's feelings are important to a nation; that shame and rejection can block a mind from learning, hence segregation is a barrier to human growth which no state in our democracy can maintain legally in its public school system.

For a little while, that day, we forgot Asia and Africa. We were thinking of children. Of their needs. Bread, books, shoes? These we have tried to give them. But to grow as human beings they must have esteem, they must have belief in their own worth and the worth of others. Now they would have a better chance to grow. Every child could begin to feel at home here, knowing he is accepted in the American family. From this time on he will be safeguarded from those who do not care: from the bullies and the haters and the sick minds and the political opportunists who, in their greed, are willing to feed on our children's future to make their own present big.

White children were not mentioned in that remarkable

document, but they too are deeply affected by it. For race segregation is a cruel frame that twists and misshapes the spirits of all children, no matter which side of it they are fastened to. Arrogance, complacency, blindness to human need: these hurt the heart and mind as severely as do shame and inferiority. We hardly need to remind ourselves of how the little Nazis' moral natures were maimed by Hitler's ideas and laws to know this is true.

White Southerners know it so well. As we listened to the decision, many of us were suddenly back in childhood, quietly walking through its years, remembering its beauty, its tender moments, its sudden joy and wonder—and its walls. Those invisible walls which we plunged against a thousand times as we stretched out to accept our human world. Walls that stopped our questions—and our dreams. We were so free . . . but we did not have the freedom to do right. For there were laws in our states that compelled us to do wrong.

Now the Supreme Court's decision would give this freedom back to the white child of the South. It is a very big gift, for which many of us are deeply grateful.

Months passed. Autumn had come. Schools once more opened. And some were for the first time in their history without segregation. The decision had made plain what the law is. The school boards decided to wait no longer. In the good American way, they went ahead on this new frontier, exploring, taking risks; with courage and independence they began to work things out.

In the border states, Delaware, West Virginia, in the

city of Baltimore, in Washington, D. C. (where there is a larger number of Negro pupils than white), the school children were learning brand-new lessons together. The most important lessons they had ever learned: that had to do with freedom and its relationship to responsibility; with the meaning of human rights; with the place of law in their personal lives. They were beginning to see that our American Constitution is the steel frame that holds this great skyscraper we call democracy firmly to the earth. They began to understand that freedom can be freedom to do wrong as easily as it can be freedom to do right—unless our country's laws are obeyed.

They were vivid lessons—for suddenly, as if in a play, they were acted out: white children struck, demanding that colored children's rights be disregarded; white parents struck, telling their children they need not respect the Constitution, they need not esteem the Supreme Court and the highest laws of our land.

There were not many strikers. Only a few thousand. But enough. Enough for us to see what it looks like when American citizens put their allegiance to their color above the Constitution of the United States. Enough for us to see what anarchy could look like; enough for us to read fresh meanings into the word "subversive."

We, the American public, were back at school now—with the children—learning again lessons we had almost forgot.

With shocking clarity, we realized that no parent or child who had a regard for human rights and love of justice could have participated in those strikes.

We began to see that we have been so busy opposing communism that we have not stopped to ask: *What does democracy mean to me? to my children? Perhaps I love it as little as a Communist does; perhaps I do not understand it any better than he. Is this true?*

We began to realize that a nation is no better than the people in it; its strength is no greater than the beliefs in their hearts and the values they hold to.

We had heard it said a thousand times. Yes. But here, suddenly, it was dramatized for us, clearly, sharply. All one had to do was look at the pictures of those strikers to realize that somehow, somewhere, we have failed—and in a big way.

We began to understand that a democracy cannot do without quality in its people—and yet it cannot give them quality. It needs goodness—there is no substitute for it—and yet it cannot make its people good.

It can only protect their right to be as good as they want to be. It can only safeguard their children's right to learn and grow toward maturity. It protects everybody —rich, poor, colored, white, well-bodied and crippled, the dull and the genius, the young, the old—but that is all it can do.

To grow good human beings is the people's business: a job that must be done in the home, at church, in school; goodness seeps into a child from the books he reads, the art he loves, his play, his talk, his dreams and ideals, his awareness of others and their needs. As we watched these school children and their parents making mistakes, learning new lessons in this time of change, we saw this clearly. And we knew we had not attended to our business well enough.

Then it was that many began to realize that this ordeal of school integration can become for the entire nation a magnificent opportunity for growth, for soul-searching, for rediscovery of important things. It can become a great moment in American history if only we have the vision to see the creative possibilities in this crisis; if only we remember that it is not ordeal that determines our future but what we do about it, what we make of it.

It is a great challenge. Perhaps our one big chance to strengthen democracy here at home. If we meet it well we shall, at last, be living our beliefs, measuring up to our responsibilities. And this knowledge, this lifting of a burden which has been on our conscience so long, will quicken our imagination and release our energies. It will enlarge our sympathies for people everywhere, who, too, are changing, who, too, are searching for something real and abiding to compose their lives around.

If we succeed, it will demonstrate to the world how change, deep change, can be brought about in a democracy without violence and bloodshed.

If we succeed, perhaps our friends across the earth will be persuaded that though we have among our rights the right to make mistakes, we feel also the obligation to correct those mistakes once we see we have made them. There is no person, no group of people, no nation, that does not make grave mistakes. The test is: can they rectify their mistake? A man's honor becomes involved in how he meets this test; his sense of responsibility for the future of his children and the human race becomes involved. Honor and responsibility are a man's and a nation's greatest assets. They will carry us through any ordeal and, in the process, will enrich us and our civilization, no matter how painful the ordeal may be.

Our founding fathers understood that always there would be need for a nation to correct its old mistakes. And because they understood, they created a Constitution that was and still is a living, growing thing: resilient, flexible, sensitive to the fact that men change as they gain knowledge of their world and of themselves. Read it: you see within its pages so many open spaces left for growth. The people can do wrong, yes; we have in the past and will again; but our Constitution holds within it the potentials for doing right and the machinery for correcting our errors—and they will be corrected as soon as enough of us realize that change is needed.

Change in a democracy can be brought about quickly or slowly. The speed depends on its people's honesty of mind, their values, their humility and knowledge and insight; and, above all else, on the will to act, once they realize the need for action.

It took a long time for enough of us to see how wrong segregation is, how injurious it is to a whole nation for a group of its children in any state to be set apart or hidden away by law because of their differences—whatever those differences may be, real or unreal.

It would have taken longer—had it not been that freedom to protest and to dream of a better life are an integral part of the American way.

From 1881 to 1907, widespread enactment of segregation laws took place in Southern states. Protests from Negroes, who dreamed of a future for their people and knew they had a right to their dreams, began in slavery and increased as the segregation laws were set up. One by one, Negroes spoke out. Then more and more spoke bravely, eloquently, in prayer, song, poetry, art, books, in organized demands for their rights, in scientific accomplishments, in sacrifices for their country—using every means of communication they could get their hands on to lay their case before the conscience of our nation.

And white people, North and South, joined them in their protests. It is a good thing to remember that never has the Negro group been alone. Always there have been white people, many of them—first in the North, then in the South—who have identified with them as human beings, giving priority not to pigmentation of skin but to the spirit of man. Americans who knew that segregation divides and weakens democracy and, if persisted in too long, will destroy it and the quality of its people.

But it was another kind of speaking out—the brilliant work of the Legal Committee of the National Association for the Advancement of Colored People—that culminated in the great decision of May seventeenth.

The Legal Committee's purpose was to find means, within the American framework of law, by which Negroes could reclaim their constitutional rights. One of its first acts was to challenge the grandfather clause in Oklahoma—a clause that tried in a shrewd, twisting way to stop Negroes from voting because they had ancestors who had been in slavery. It won its case.

It proceeded to test the constitutionality of other segregation statutes. The white primary is one of the most famed.

As time has passed, as case after case has been hung up in the public mind to be looked at, the American people have grown increasingly aware of the deep wounds which the act of segregation inflicts on the human spirit.

Throughout the years the NAACP has been criticized, sneered at, called "communist" by many who seem not to know, or to have forgotten, how their own government works: what rights a citizen is guaranteed by our Constitution; what legal procedures may be used to get back his rights when they have been taken from him.

How else, except through peaceful protest, and the courts, can change come about in our country? We have no dictator to make us change. We do not resort to revolution. A democracy cannot stay alive if the people in it do not urge change when change is necessary; it cannot grow unless the people have vision. Therefore, reformers, prophets, poets, and protest groups belong to the democratic way of life. If a man does not like them, he does not like democracy.

The entire work of the Legal Committee of the NAACP will, I believe, go down in history as a superb example of the American way of correcting wrongs in a spirit of reason and good will.

It will show that this process of bringing about change in laws, or deciding on the validity of old laws, is also an important means of educating the people whom these laws affect; and that the Supreme Court, our highest authority, bases its decisions not only on the Constitution and legal precedents but on its and the people's awareness of the necessities of their times.

"The inn that shelters for the night is not the journey's end," said Justice Benjamin Cardozo. "The law, like the traveler, must be ready for the morrow. It must have the principle of growth."

The Supreme Court has made its decision. Will it become ours also? Will we put it into effect quickly enough, harmoniously enough, for it to be the means of revitalizing our own faith and restoring the world's confidence in our integrity?

This is the unanswered question.

There is so much to give us hope. The timing of the decision was so right. It is in the full current of history; it had to come—even those hostile to the decision admit that this change is an inevitable one. It is right for our children, right in terms of scientific knowledge, right for our nation's integrity, right for world peace.

And we have fabulous resources for bringing it about: instant, nationwide communication by television, radio, newspapers; we have facts, techniques; there are many responsible, skilled people who are deeply concerned, who understand the urgent need of a quiet, immediate acceptance of this decision, and who can communicate their understanding to the people. As a nation we are prospering; no heavy economic pressures are on us; the South's old one-crop system of agriculture which, for so long, made exploitation of the Negro group profitable to many has almost disappeared—and with it one motivation for "keeping things as they are." There is a strong bond of good will and understanding between the two races, especially in the South, where there have always been many warm personal relationships. It is well to remind ourselves of this; to keep clear the fact that white Southerners do not hate Negroes. There are the haters, yes, who vent their hatred on whomever society permits them to; but though they have loud voices, they are limited in number.

Then what is holding us back?

Two things: anxiety—a taboo-like fear—which is aroused in many minds when the pattern of segregation is questioned; and the demagogues and other opportunists who deliberately exploit this anxiety to their political and economic advantage.

It may be wise to forget these opportunists for a little while and look hard at the fear.

The majority of Americans do not dread integration; but there are some who do. To many of these, South and North, the giving up of segregation seems a very hard thing; and to a few it is a terrifying disaster.

Why?

❖ 2 ❖

LET US search for the roots of this fear not in the word *Negro* but in the word *segregation*. Turn it slowly.

It has many synonyms: *isolation, censorship, restriction, withdrawal, Jim Crow, caste, imprisonment, quarantine, repression,* are only a few. Each has a special meaning, a different purpose, but the act and the need are the same: we hide a part of the world from us because we want to make our own lives more secure.

The danger we fear may be real or unreal, inside us or outside, small or large. No matter. When it threatens us, we block it off if we have no better defense to use.

We do it by locking our doors or locking our minds; by hiding in caves or in dreams; by climbing trees, building walls, putting up signs, or hanging iron curtains; and sometimes by making laws that separate us from what we want and dread to be near.

The human language is full of our hiding places—and full of the ways in which we have made them.

For segregation is our oldest defense. One each of us begins to use early in life. One we keep using for there are times when nothing else works, and times, also, when our consciences will not let us use anything else.

And, if we know when and how to use it, it is, even today, an effective defense and an honorable one.

Let us turn *segregation* again.

It has been used since man's earliest days to protect him from danger, but it is used also for creative purposes. An artist segregates himself from his world in order to bring back to it a gift: a poem, a picture, a book, a carving, a symphony. A mystic retires to his cloister to meditate on God, and, in the doing of it, to find deeper meanings to share with his fellow men. A scientist stays in his laboratory so that he may concentrate on his search for new knowledge, which, later, becomes the common possession of all men. The young are secluded in schools in order to learn more about one another and the world around them. The sick are hospitalized in order to be cured. Those with contagious diseases, or those who are violently disturbed, are quarantined so they may be healed and the rest of us protected. A disaster area is wired off for the purpose of giving immediate first aid.

Segregation measures like these are necessities. One cannot conceive of a civilized world without them. They fit completely the nature of man because they are, for the most part, freely accepted; their purpose is creative; their results are enriching to the one segregated and to his world; and their duration is limited.

But, regardless of its purpose, what happens when segregation is used too long? What does permanent isolation do to a community, a nation? What does it do to an artist, a scientist? What happens to a child's feelings when he is cut off too long from his human world? When is "too long"?

These are questions we rarely ask. And yet they are

the heart of the matter. It is meaningless to ask, "Is segregation wrong? Is it right?" For it can be wrong or right depending on the *length of time it is used*. However valid its purpose, however creative, however freely entered into, it becomes wrong *when used too long*.

Time is of the essence of this problem—as it is of most human problems.

How long can a man be deprived of air without dying? How long can he stay under water? How long can he go without food and drink? How long can he endure extreme cold, extreme heat? How long can he bleed? These are old, familiar questions. They make sense. A man needs air, food, water, blood, a moderate temperature, and will die without them.

How long can a child be cut off from the community without harm to him? How long can a nation be isolated from the rest of the world? How long can a democracy segregate a group of its citizens without destroying its own integrity? These questions, too, make sense.

For man becomes human and is kept so by his relationships with his human world and by his ties to past and future. Cut him off from his memories—who is he? Cut him off from his dreams—what keeps his hope alive? Cut him off from knowledge—what happens to his mind? Break his ties with his fellow men—what happens to his feelings? Destroy his belief in God, in something bigger than himself, something more important—what happens to his growth and his goodness?

We are learning the answers. We are becoming more

aware of the significance for each of us of that phrase, *man's relationships.*

We know, now, that the spirit of a child, isolated from his human world, shrinks and dies quickly because it has too little tenderness and esteem to feed on. We understand that an artist who withdraws permanently will stop creating because his dreams die when no longer fed on fresh human relationships; a scientist who has cut himself off from men will lose touch with the moral center of that universe he seeks knowledge of; a mystic in his retreat will not find God if he has lost contact with God's children. We see quite plainly now that barbed wire put up to stay is no first-aid station but a concentration camp; that an iron curtain harms the people behind it more than those in front of it.

We know this: because we know that men cannot do without each other. Animals may go it alone. Men cannot do so. Genius or retarded child or ordinary man, sick or well, rich or poor, white or colored, Westerner or Asian—however different or alike we may be, we need each other. We belong together.

As babies we grew into humanness because of the care and tenderness given us by other human beings. As mature men and women we stay human and grow in stature because we are nourished on each other's esteem and acceptance and concern. Whatever we learn stems from another man's knowledge; whatever we discover is but a smidge added on to the discoveries of a million others; whatever understanding we have of life comes because men who lived and died before we were born revealed themselves honestly to their world; whatever we know of humility we learned because some one forgave our mistakes; whatever hope we have is ours because of the fortitude and faith and honor of others. Whatever lies ahead in the human future is there because men—yesterday, today, a thousand or ten thousand years ago—have had a vision of what our world can become and shared their vision with us.

Do we deserve so much? Of course not. *Deserve* is not a relevant word to use about human beings. No one of us—child or grownup, man or woman, intelligent or dull, good or bad, white or colored—"deserves" what we have received since the day we were born.

We do not deserve but we *need* each other's concern and acceptance and the world's rich gifts. And our world needs what we can freely give in return, and give in our own way.

Out of these interwoven needs and fulfillments is made the fabulous fabric we call human life. All morality is based on its central truth: *that men in their different ways must meet each other's needs, and in the doing of it will find a larger, a freer life for themselves.*

When we hold to this image of the human being—this creature called man, who is so helpless and weak when alone, and so strong in his numberless ties and relationships; this man who must be free and yet, at the same time, depends on others and is depended upon, who must be allowed his differences and yet shares in a common humanity and a common future—when we see this image clearly, this human being nourished on a million relationships, we begin to understand how profoundly immoral is segregation whenever it is of long-time duration, and whenever it is deliberately used as a knife to cut a man's ties in two.

We have used that knife, as individuals or as groups, only when we were desperate and knew nothing else to do.

Turn the pages of history or of your own life: you find that men have never casually segregated themselves or others for a long period of time. It is true, they have done so, in the name of this difference or that. But *always extreme anxiety compelled them to commit this anti-human act;* and always the results have been destructive. There is something in us that knows better. Call it sanity or morality or the will to survive: a wisdom lies deep in every healthy personality, urging it to keep related to the human world.

❖ 3 ❖

LET US look at *segregation* again.

To many, today, the word means only *color barrier*. When it is said, things turn black and white.

It may be wise, therefore, to remind ourselves of a fact we know but often forget: that, long before white people and colored people saw each other, we segregated members of our families, and our neighbors.

Why? Because some of them were different from us, and their differences frightened us.

No Negro in America today is as severely cut off from his world as were the deaf and blind until the twentieth century; nor is he as discriminated against as were, until recent decades, those with cerebral palsy, the mentally ill, and many others disabled or different in body or mind.

For countless generations, no one believed a deaf child could speak. We called him "deaf and dumb." We not only thought him a natural mute, we doubted his good sense. There are recorded instances in the sixteenth and seventeenth centuries of the deaf being refused communion in the church because they "probably have no souls." The blind, throughout most of human history, have been beggars and outcasts, herded together, pushed back in alleys in the cities, often with no roof over their heads. They were refused schooling. They were not taught to work. No effort, save in rare cases, was made to help them find a human place in the community. The child or grownup with epilepsy was "possessed" by devils; his brains would "waste away." No attempt was made to educate him, although he was no different from others in his intelligence; no work was offered him; and for him to marry was an outrage, although the chances of transmission of epilepsy through inheritance are low. (There are in eighteen states, even now, laws against marriage of epileptics, and in many states laws forbid their attendance at public school.) The person with cerebral palsy—the spastic—was called an "idiot" by many, and few dreamed he could learn, although from 65 to 70 per cent of these birth-injured children have normal or above normal intelligence. The mentally ill were called "crazy" and were often chained in dungeon-like places, often whipped or imprisoned; and no one thought they could recover their peace of mind and take their place again in their human world.

To make things worse, books were written in the eighteenth century (best sellers they were, too) which claimed that "secret sins" caused all these troubles and more: they caused tuberculosis also, and diarrhea, constipation, cancer, and what have you.

And people believed these fantastic statements. What else was there to believe? We were so ignorant. Most people were illiterate. Knowledge was accumulating slowly and there were few means of communicating the little we knew. No machine age was in sight. Few techniques, almost no instruments, had been invented for gaining precise knowledge. What our learned men knew was mainly concerned with the world outside themselves. They understood almost nothing about the human body and mind. The exteriors of our bodies were plain, everyday facts; their interiors were a mystery and at times felt like haunted houses—so full were they of feelings we did not understand, fears we could not name. impulses we had no control over, and diseases that killed us off quickly or left us twisted and maimed.

Today, scientific knowledge has turned most of those giant mysteries into clear realities. Rehabilitation, working hand in hand with science, has given new hope to the disabled. The discovery of antibiotics and other new drugs has given cures for diseases. But for so long we did not have facts and rehabilitation, techniques and antibiotics: we had only a terrible need to understand why so much trouble befell us. And in our hunger to find meaning in our ordeal we asked the wrong questions: *Who is to blame, our own secret sins or the sins of our fathers?* Or sometimes we asked the most hurting question of all: *Why did God do this to me?*

Then it was that the little truth and the big lie mated, the superstition and the whisper, the old wives' tale and the parental threat, until a brood of fantastic, distorted images filled our minds. Deeply anxious, feeling a guilt whose cause we did not know, we hid away the disabled and different, even those of our own family, hoping to rid ourselves of the awful burden that mystery and misinformation had laid upon us.

There was nothing else we could think of to do. Our other defenses in those days were too crude, too feeble for so large a trouble.

But even in those dark times there were the few who said, "These different ones are human too. There is a way to relate them to our world if we search for it. And we must find it; for we need them as much as they need us."

Always they come—the ones with the vision, the faith, the profound understanding of what makes men human and keeps them so. Always they remind us that we must not only tolerate one another's differences, we must treasure them; for out of these differences come the unpredictable, the new idea, the bright dream, the strange and wondrous gift. When times grow dark, when we persecute or hide away others because of our fears, these few turn the lights on again with their words. Whether they speak in the name of religion, science, or common decency, their concern causes miracles to happen: men begin to lose their fear, they find things to do, they discover within themselves potentialities they did not know they possessed; and, making use of them, they move the human race up a little—a few inches, at least—to a higher level of feeling and doing, learning and becoming.

It is a good thing to remember that never have all the lights gone out, no matter how confused and bewildered an age we live in. Always there have been those whose vision stayed clear.

In the twentieth century, there have been thousands in America, Europe, Asia, who not only have had faith and hope and vision but, with the resources of science, have found more and more things to do. Especially have the millions of disabled been helped. They are beginning now to live whole lives; they are making their rightful place in our world. No demagogue (except Hitler) has dared exploit them. Walls hiding them away did not harden into laws, nor did their differences become a controversial issue which politicians could use as a means of gaining personal power. Nor did the public make money off them. And because these things did not happen, our attitude—once we had the facts, once we knew things to do—changed quickly toward the millions whom we hid away for so many centuries.

And yet, even now, there are some who do not accept the disabled, who will not employ them, who do not think they should go to school with "normal" children, who still try not to see.

Segregation of the maimed and the different was too easy to use; we used it too long. For centuries it shut them away. It helped us forget what we did not want to think about and thereby lessened our anxiety. But it shut us away too, from the deep springs of compassion which keep alive our concern for others, and from the love of truth which sharpens our talent for asking new questions.

We paid a costly defense bill for a false security.

As we think back through human history, we see how often we have used segregation not against "real" dangers but to ease our fears.

We have used it against the stranger, against members of our own families, against those who have a different religion or different beliefs, and sometimes against ourselves when the different parts of our natures do not harmonize.

Is it, then, men's differences that we fear?

I do not think so. We fear those who are different only when they become, for an extraneous reason, a threat to us. The threat may be real or a made-up thing. There was nothing real to fear in the blind or the epileptic. What harm could they do us? They were not our economic competitors; they could not injure us; they had no way to dominate us. *They* were not the threat. The threat lay in the false ideas we had about them, in the conflict within us which these ideas set up, in the dread that "something bad might happen to us too"; in the guilty feeling that "maybe their trouble is the family's fault."

❖ 4 ❖

LET US look now at segregation as it has been used against the colored people.

It is an interesting fact that the white race felt no fear and little dislike of colored people when they first came in contact with them. The dark color of their skin aroused anxiety no more than did dark hair or dark eyes. It was different, yes. But neither literature nor history reveals the existence of any real race prejudice in the Western world until about two centuries ago.

Colored people held no threat for us. They did not—as did the disabled—remind us of what "might happen to us." They were not as yet an embodiment of "somebody's sin." They were a bit strange to look at, it is true. But they were strong, well formed, intelligent, with their full share of beauty and vigor and charm—human beings who aroused interest, not panic.

Then something began to happen.

Three centuries ago, the European powers invaded Asia and Africa. Slowly they conquered and colonized vast areas of these continents. By force, by peaceful trickery, they secured the spices and tea they needed, the raw materials they sought, the new markets for commerce. They found also an unexpected and highly profitable commodity for trade: human beings who were different. Their bodies were fine and strong; they were bright enough; but their skin was dark, they spoke a different language, they were not Christians, and, in the tropical heat, did not wear many clothes. Maybe this means, the trader's ignorant, greedy mind whispered, that it is all right to enslave them. He did so. It was not too difficult to kidnap them, for they had been bred in a culture that made them trustful. Once they were kidnaped, the trader piled them in sailing vessels and hauled those who survived to America, or sometimes to seaports of England and Portugal or Spain, where they were resold to the colonies.

They brought a fine price. The developing plantations in the South needed cheap labor. Free labor was better. The demand grew. Buying and selling of colored human beings mushroomed into big business. Great family fortunes were built on it in Europe, in New England, in New York; and in the South the plantation system, which these slaves made possible, flourished.

But as European nations grew powerful from a "white" colonialism that had begun to encircle the globe; as the young, free United States, once a colony herself, now began to profit from slavery; as these intertwining systems of slavery in America and colonialism in Asia and Africa became deeply rooted in our Western lives, the white man's feelings changed toward those who were colored. He grew anxious.

What caused his anxiety?

It came, as we are beginning to see plainly, from the

profound conflict between his Christian beliefs and slavery. It was sharpened to a razor edge by the never-ending debate between the idea of democracy and the act of colonialism. It was made worse by the jagged fact of the white man's back-yard sex relationships in Asia, in Africa, in our own country. These conflicts, which concerned our deepest beliefs and most cherished dreams and our everyday way of making money, troubled most thoughtful persons in the Western world.

The white race believed in freedom. The Western world had stated the case for human dignity and equal rights more brilliantly and convincingly than had any other people on earth. The United States was founded on these beliefs. Our Constitution, our Bill of Rights, our laws, made them plain, concrete facts. And, as these political ideas grew into a way of life, Christians began to speak more clearly than ever before their belief in brotherhood, in the importance of children, the dignity of women and of motherhood. Pity, compassion, concern, were feelings men felt and words they used and esteemed. And the more they used these words and felt these emotions, the more anxious they grew, for they could not forget what they were doing to the colored people and to themselves.

For the Western world, slavery and colonialism and the cheapened relationships they brought with them had come a thousand years too late. There was no way to square them with the new age we were beginning to live in.

The Christian religion, with roots deep in Judaic culture, had changed these Western "barbarians"—as the world once called us—into thoughtful human beings who valued knowledge, who could feel anger and do violent things, yes, but who knew also the meaning of mercy and forgiveness. Christianity had given men ideas about the worth of the human being never dreamed of before. "A new commandment I give unto you, that ye love one another," its Founder had said and dramatized in His life and death. Slowly that commandment had grown in meaning for men, seeping through their minds and their lives.

By the eighteenth century it had fused with ideas that had come to us from the Greeks, the Romans, and was flowering into phrases like *freedom of man, human rights, democracy, liberty, equal opportunity, justice*.

Exciting ideas. Once hearing them, a man could not keep them to himself. He saw doors opening, a new age emerging—*his* age. He wanted to be a part of it. More and more heard of the ideas. More and more began to hunger for freedom and to ask, "What are *my* rights?"

Almost by the sheer magic of their words, men had moved their human world up to another level where each man counted as a person, where tyranny was everybody's foe—and suddenly something evil in us, something greedy and terrible, had begun to pull it down again. It is true we did not have as yet the means to implement these dreams; we could not make them come true for all people everywhere. Even so, we knew there was no place for slavery, no room for colonialism, in this new age of freedom.

We were torn to pieces. Here was a moral problem, an earth-sized ambiguity, that would give our souls and our world no peace until it was solved.

And yet we white people did not want to solve it. We did not want to because it profited the few in money and power, and all white people in prestige, not to. We knew we could not believe in both freedom and slavery; we knew we could not glorify the home and cheapen womanhood and childhood in the back yards of the world; we knew we could not be loyal to both colonialism and democracy. But we tried.

As the years passed, the moral conflict grew worse. Voices, inside us and outside, were critical.

To stem our guilt, we began to defend the indefensible: we declared that God had made the white race superior to other races—and thereby tried to justify our exploitation of darker men. We talked and wrote nonsense about "purity of blood" and the "best" culture and "best" civilization, as if morals and art and science, inventions and wisdom, ran through one's bloodstream or were filed away in one's genes; as if a civilization could grow with no relationship to the world civilization that has been growing since the beginning of man. We talked about "the heathen" so we would not see our own sins. We spoke of "backward people" so we would not have to face the big backward step we had taken as a Christian people. These things were said not only in the South. Wherever there were white people who were colonizing darker people or enslaving them or profiting from their exploitation, such talk took place.

The long cold war with our conscience had begun.

Perhaps we should not blame our old grandfathers too much. They lived in a time of ignorance, when there were few facts about genetics or cultures, or the human body and mind. No one knew the real reasons why pigmentation of the skin differs in different parts of the earth; the effects of thousands of years of climate and food and inbreeding had not been studied. There were, as yet, no means, no techniques for acquiring such knowledge. And so, in their guilty need to justify what could not be justified, they fell back on superstitions and old wives' tales, on half-truths and whole lies—piling up these verbal defenses until they had walled themselves away from what they could not bear to see.

Now they had a vested interest in ignorance. It would not be easy to give up this ignorance later, when science came with its knowledge—not nearly as easy as it would be to slough off the old superstitions and accept new knowledge about disease and the disabled.

In the midst of that cold war with our conscience came a civil war in the United States, which ended legal slavery forever in our nation.

But it did not make for peace of mind. Moral problems are not often settled by wars. The bitter Reconstruction which followed the war, though it helped Negroes a little, made new difficulties—economic, political, spiritual —for both races. Finally the South reached a level of misery and resentment and hurt where criticism could not help. The people needed encouragement, practical aid, a "Point Four program." They needed to see doors opening for all the people, white and colored. But for a long time they received little aid of any kind.

It is painful to look at the giant problems that confronted our grandfathers, and at the unwise decisions they made. And yet we cannot understand our own moment in history if we do not understand theirs. We need, above all else, to keep in mind the context in which they made their mistakes.

Today, when political opportunists talk about "tradition," when they demand that we repeat the mistakes our grandparents made, they brush off a very big fact that we need to hold on to: *we are not living in the world our grandparents lived in.* Today we have so much that they lacked: means of communication, skills, machines, prosperity, knowledge, and a clear sense of the interdependence of all people. What could not be done by them in a year or five years we often do now in a day. Pressures have lifted, cultural patterns have changed, no economic motivation exists today for the peonage they once felt they could not do without. Our world has changed, and our minds and consciences have changed too. It is insulting to our grandparents to assume that, were they living today, *in our age,* they would make the same mistakes they made in theirs. They were caught in a trap that does not exist now. And yet the demagogues are trying hard to hypnotize the people into believing it is still here, urging them to go find it and crawl into it and repeat the old tragic errors of long ago.

It was during those troubled times that demagoguery got its big start in the South. We desperately needed leaders with vision to help find exits from a trouble that was crowding the people hard. Such leaders did not appear. Instead, the demagogues came, crying "Fire! Fire!"—and closing the doors against our escape.

❖ 5 ❖

TO UNDERSTAND how these demagogues exploited our grandparents' dilemma, how they fattened on old fears, we must go back a few steps to that hurting word *Reconstruction*.

Even now the word can bring back to us—who were not born then and know it only from family stories and history books—a dread picture of chaos, terror, humiliation, and grief.

That time has gone forever. But memories do not die so long as they have feelings to feed on. They live from generation to generation. Children may forget the "facts," false or true, or never learn them—but they remember their parents' feelings, and keep remembering, until those feelings become their own.

The war, the South's defeat, the ineffectual methods used by the federal "reconstructors," had left our region full of displaced persons without homes, jobs, or status, with a past already blurring, with feelings too restlessly charged with the right and wrong of their experiences to be brought into equilibrium. All our people, white and colored, had had too many of their personal relationships cut sharply in two, too many daily routines and rituals torn to shreds, to find easily again serenity and harmony.

During that tragic, chaotic era our grandfathers first used, in a widespread way, race segregation, setting it up as a civic defense—much as we stretch barbed wire today, after disaster.

In each local situation, restrictions were put up hastily, and in different ways, to ease panic. Done, the white people said, "to protect the women folks" from homeless, rootless ex-slaves who might go berserk; done also, they said, "to protect the colored folks" from half-crazed white men who might expend on them the resentment they felt toward their northern "enemies." Responsible men in the communities, on the farms, knew the haters and hotheads, knew that in such chaos a chain reaction of terror and violence could easily be set off. One has only to remember that there were no electric lights, no paved roads, no telephones, few cities and towns, many swamps and forests, to realize the added pressures that distance and darkness laid on the people.

Looked at as an emergency measure, the *temporary use* of segregation in that time and place was an act of plain common sense. It gave a pattern and order that the federal troops had not achieved. It said, *You go this way; you go that way.* There was little cruelty in these early orders, little desire to shame or humiliate anyone. All most people wanted in those unhappy days was security and peace—and food.

As the years went by, things quieted down. The federal troops departed. The Northerners went back home— or remained to become our wealthiest citizens (for there were ways to make money from our misery).

Times were still hard: jobs were scarce, wages were almost at starvation level for everybody; industry was weak and there was little of it; sharecropping, perhaps worse in many ways than slavery, was the only answer farm owners of our region had found; credit was being re-established, though interest rates were high and the moneylenders—as in every impoverished rural region in the world—were, for the most part, opportunists and parasites.

Even so, things were leveling off. Order had come. Law had been re-established. Negroes and whites had settled down somewhere. The region was slowly regaining its political place in the nation's affairs. Health and public schools and wealth were beginning to come—at least to the few.

Then was the time for leaders to come forward and say, "Let us put away self-pity. We have been through severe ordeal; we cannot help that; but its meaning for us depends on our attitude toward it. Let us stop feeling persecuted, stop looking at a past gone forever, stop spreading rumors; let us make of our region a good place for all the people to live in; let us develop its rich human resources as well as its land and forest and minerals and water; let us accept each other as free citizens; let us live our private lives as we wish, but take care that we protect every man's public rights." But not one leader said this.

Then was the time to take down the emergency measures of race segregation. But it was already too late.

The politicians had picked up "the Negro issue" like a football and were tossing the destiny of millions back and forth in their political games.

Poverty? They took it for granted; they defended sharecropping—and low wages; fought unions when unions came to the South.

The children? Neither politicians nor voters thought much, in those days, of what happens to a child's growth when his feelings are twisted and shamed. To them, the "race issue" did not concern human beings. It was the ball in a game called *politics*—a game as cruel as the old Roman arena sports, and sometimes as wildly enjoyed by the people. Morals had no place in it, nor fair play, nor integrity.

A few of the more sensitive and intelligent politicians disliked to play this game. They hated the corruption, the vulgarity, the sensationalism of the race issue. Even so—as many do today—they justified their acts by saying, "It is the only way you can get elected."

The race issue was used, roughly, in this fashion: One politician outsmarted his rival by slapping the poll tax on his state's lawbooks. His opponent retaliated by bloc-voting the Negroes. This led to fresh retaliation.

The first one who could, put further restrictions on voting by setting up "literacy tests" (which could be bypassed by most whites, through the quickly enacted "grandfather clause," which exempted an illiterate from the test if his grandfather had voted). So it went, each building power for himself and his machine by reducing the number of people who could vote—and doing it in any way he could.

But politicians, powerful as they are, cannot write poll-tax laws and grandfather clauses on a state's lawbooks—not in a democracy. The people must put them there. To persuade them to do so, fears must first be aroused. So the demagogues got busy. They drilled with their electric lies deep into our memories, stirring up the unhappy past, telling ghost stories about "race dangers," seasoning their barbecue speeches with obscene innuendoes about "mongrelizing," about "your sister marrying a Negro," and sadistic phrases: *rivers of blood . . . troops with bayonets . . . invasion of the home.*

Then what happened? More lynchings—naturally. For the mentally unstable (white and colored) were aroused by such speeches and did violent, foolish things, hardly knowing why they did them.

Immediately after a lynching, more segregation statutes were put on lawbooks to "control racial violence." Signs went over doors, over drinking fountains; public buildings were often out of bounds to Negroes. Jim Crow travel cars were set up—hooked onto trains going South at Washington, D. C. Eating together in restaurants and in trains in the South was banned.

This was happening in a group of states in the freest country on earth. Those states were, as time passed, pleasant places to live in, for white people; calm on the surface, for black people; almost no brutality was seen on streets or in public places; laughter and easy, friendly talk were shared by whites and blacks in the stores, and in the homes where the colored people were in domestic service; errands of mercy were done by members of both races for each other. You could live in a Southern town for ten years and perhaps never see one violent act occur between members of the two races. And yet—

Like a cancer in a strong, vital body, race segregation —and the arrogance and shame and obscenity and corruption and censorship that accompany it—had begun its deadly growth, spreading through minds and homes, creeping into churches, into schools, into the newspapers, into books, dulling our concern for one another, destroying our love of truth and our tenderest beliefs. Suddenly it would appear in a distant place, in another—until, finally, in twenty-one of our forty-eight states there were legal race barriers; and in the others feelings hardened into gentlemen's agreements which began to write housing covenants, to create ghettos, to restrict hotels and restaurants, to determine what was said about segregation and intermarriage in magazines with national circulation—and, later, in motion pictures—to set up barriers in fraternities in Northern universities and in professional societies.

As signs went up over doors in the South, they went

up almost as quickly over minds in the North. For race segregation was beginning to pay profits—economic, political, psychological—not only in Dixie but throughout the United States.

We cannot, even yet, assess the harm done by the walls that were put up in minds, North and South. We can see more clearly the consequences of the legal barriers.

The poll tax, put on Southern statute books to "keep Negroes from voting," kept white people from voting too. The white primary, set up to maintain "white supremacy," maintained white political machines also—machines which are today fueled and refueled by the word "segregation." Segregated public schools, so costly to support that they could not be kept at a level of efficiency, kept most of the people ignorant. Segregated state universities increased the costs and decreased the quality of higher education. The county-unit system in Georgia, by limiting the people's ballots to county-unit votes in the primaries (which are equivalent in Georgia to election), virtually took away the people's voting franchise. (For the smallest county of 3000 people is given two unit votes, while the largest county of 500,000 is given six votes.) Dual systems of parks, of public rest rooms, libraries, hospitals, penal institutions, loaded the taxpayers with public debts they could ill afford to pay. The Negroes suffered most from this separate-but-never-equal system. But the whites suffered also.

These measures, which deprived all the people of some

of their rights and opportunities, were put on statute books at times when the demagogues had whipped our feelings into panic.

The Christians, the people of good will—how did they feel when segregation was made compulsory?

They were relieved.

The moral conflict had lasted so long. Conscience had been raw and hurting through endless years. Legal segregation, spurious as it was, made people feel that, from here on out, there was nothing they could do about it. Even though compulsory segregation took away their freedom to do right, it "settled things."

Had the church only spoken out while these laws were being passed. Had one bishop, one priest, one prominent preacher in each Southern state taken a bold stand against this desecration of the human spirit. How often we have said this to one another during recent years! For we know if only a few had done so, in our parents' and grandparents' time, our problems would be different today. If a handful of newspapers editors had protested, if a few statesmen had come forward, if one thoughtful citizen in each town, each county, had raised questions as to where this panic was leading us—the demagogic holocaust might have been stopped. The power of integrity and truth is so strong: even a few speaking out at a critical time can close off the wrong path and start men on the right one.

Only two well-known Southerners, from 1865 to the 1920s, did so.

One was General Robert E. Lee. He showed how he felt not often in words but again and again in his quiet acts. There was the Sunday, in early Reconstruction days, when he took communion with a Negro. In a few churches the Negroes had not, as yet, been asked to withdraw into their own churches. Communion time had come. The Negro church member went to the altar. The white Christians were confused, resentful, and stayed in their pews. There was one moment of moral blankness. Then General Lee quietly arose, walked up the aisle, knelt beside the Negro. Again and again, by his acts, he spoke plainly his beliefs in the dignity of men and the importance of their human relations. The South has never quite forgot.

And there was George Washington Cable, a young novelist who fought in the Civil War. Afterward, down in New Orleans, he wrote and said many wise things about human rights. He kept saying them. There were his memorable speech at the University of Mississippi, his letters to the newspapers. But few listened. In the 1880s, deeply discouraged, he left the South and spent the rest of his days in New England, believing his words had been wasted. But here, there, a young white Southerner read them, a young Northerner, a young Negro—and remembered.

After his voice hushed, there was no other.

Many abhorred violence and did things to keep it down, were dismayed at the hate and tried to teach their children not to be haters, kept their personal relationships with Negroes a kindly thing. But they did not speak out.

Nor would they let others speak. Their precarious moral equilibrium could be maintained only if no one questioned what had been done.

To keep from seeing, we, in the South, walled ourselves away from critics. We walled ourselves away from science too, when it told us things we did not want to know. We did not ban books often; we simply refused to read them if they reminded us of what we were trying to forget. We discouraged intellectual honesty in our young people by derision and threat. It was not good form to ask questions about our way of life, and we punished those who did so in quiet, subtle ways. If teachers or ministers forgot and discussed these matters in classroom or pulpit, we saw to it that they lost their posts. We were now not only segregating Negroes from whites, we were segregating ourselves from our world, shutting minds and hearts away from all that would give us insight and knowledge—still trying, as our great-grandfathers had done, to defend the morally indefensible.

During this silent time, the consciences of gentle people went to sleep. They could still be disturbed about evil in many areas of life, and were. But this evil, this injury which segregation inflicts on both the colored and the white groups, they could not bear to look at.

It was a long sleep and a troubled one.

❖ 6 ❖

DURING the early decades of the twentieth century, our parents taught my generation in the South to observe segregation. The teaching was brusque, even vulgar, in some homes. In others, it was quiet and well bred.

Those of us who lived in the latter homes learned our lessons of segregation along with our lessons of brotherhood and democracy. We learned them well; but of the three, we knew that segregation came first.

There were ideals we must value also: truth and tenderness, courtesy, and good will and hospitality. But segregation came first. Outside the home, it also came first: in church it came before brotherhood; in schools, before knowledge. Other rules might be questioned. We might (as we did), in the years after the First World War, swiftly discard old customs of behavior and dress; but segregation was not discarded. We knew we must never change it. We must never question it. How does it fit in with democracy? Don't think. With brotherhood? Don't think. With a changing world? Don't think. With the growth of a child's moral nature? Think gently and pleasantly of other things.

If we had only been able to do so!

But we lived in a democracy, whether we thought about it or not. And we loved it. We were proud of our Bill of Rights and our Constitution, even though some of us had never read them. It was good to be free. We could not help but want to share this freedom with others and were shamed that we could not do so. We went to church. We remembered brotherhood even though there was little of it there. We were not at peace with our souls when we walked out of church on Sundays: we were disturbed, restless. So little was said there, in our youth, about important things. We tried to think, Oh, well, maybe it doesn't matter; freedom, brotherhood, human dignity, integrity, poverty, little children— maybe none of it matters.

But it did matter. It is hard for the young to stop thinking and yearning for a better life; hard for them to stop trying to fit the pieces of their world together into something that makes sense—something that gives beauty and significance to human experience.

It was too hard for some of us to accept. We were young and restless, and we climbed over those walls our parents had put up in our minds. There were books— and we knew how to read; science was discovering ten thousand facts that concerned us, and we learned them; we traveled (for there were wars and many were sent across the seas); we saw things, heard things; we felt, we dreamed.

And we changed. So secretly, so slowly. But we changed. How many? Thousands of us. Millions, maybe. I do not know. Nor does anyone. For though we changed, though we no longer felt superior to others, no longer wanted more rights than citizens of other color had, though we had begun now to cherish integrity, had begun to feel a concern for the whole world, we still meekly obeyed the segregation laws we despised and knew were un-Christian and un-American.

And we remained silent. Silence was our gift to the demagogue. Year after year, we gave him this large present. We laughed at demagoguery; we were secretly outraged by it; we knew the demagogue was a disgrace and a danger to our region and our nation and our world—but each year we underwrote his activities with our silence.

Each, in his loneliness, feeling too weak to speak out. Each thinking he was the only one who did not like segregation.

We did not realize that our fellow Southerners were changing too; that the whole world was changing; that everywhere people were stirring, asking new questions, growing more and more proud of their human status. And yet, though we did not see plainly the bonds, woven of men's dreams and scientific knowledge, that were pulling us all closer and closer together—we felt them.

We knew something was happening. The current of history was flowing swiftly now toward wholeness. And we had finally, somehow, got in it. The walls were crumbling fast; distance, ignorance, language—all these were giving way. Men were becoming aware of their need of one another, increasingly sure they could not go it alone. Isolation was a defense no better than putting a log across a stream in flood: however wistfully the word might be clung to, its validity in world affairs and in our own had gone forever.

The human race, separated so long, is headed straight for a family reunion—and we dimly knew it. There is no way to stop its coming together. There are ways to protect the members' freedom and integrity, ways to restrain a greedy brother who attempts to set himself up as the police "father," ways to protect the weak from the strong who try to seat them at the second table or forbid them the front door, ways to safeguard everyone's human rights. But there is no way to stop the race of men from sharing one future. The decision is ours only as to whether that future be democratic and free or a massive tyranny.

This we were feeling down in Dixie—as were millions all over the earth.

One day, one year—no one knows the exact date—Southerners broke their silence.

Only a whisper at first. A few groups met and talked things over. Here, there, a novel questioned the old way of life. A few churchwomen began to work against lynching. Now and then a young minister preached a sermon about brotherhood—cautiously, perhaps, but he did it.

Suddenly the New Deal had come to the South and brought new hope with it. The beginnings of a new prosperity could be dimly seen. The old, deeply entrenched poverty and ignorance were giving way. Pressures were lifting. The federal government's concern for our health, our schools, our rural needs, our widespread economic problems, encouraged everybody—except the few who actually profited the most from it. (These are the ones who, today, still curse the New Deal that paid their depression debts and set them on the road to prosperity, the ones who call the TVA "creeping socialism"—this dramatic example of what people can do when they and their government work together to rehabilitate a region by using its natural resources and its people; this project which, in the eyes of the world, is the finest symbol of American democracy, working.)

Negroes were moving North. White Southerners were leaving also. But we who stayed home were moving around too: looking up and saying *howdy* to folks we had never seen before—on the street, in the alley, or out in the country. Suddenly we were meeting with Negroes —not as employers and employed, but as plain human beings. We hardly knew how it happened. But here, there, it happened.

Democracy was growing again, putting out new green shoots, sloughing off the old deadness.

Negroes were beginning to secure their rights by protesting in the good American way. Since 1909 the NAACP had existed, and had been telling the entire country of the Negro group's needs. But only now did the South really hear them. Suddenly we were listening and respecting them for boldly asking for what was due them. People began to talk about the "white Negro," Walter White, who dramatized by his brave, personal investigations the tragedy of lynching.

Then came that little pamphlet, issued in Roosevelt's second administration, called *The South: The Nation's Economic Problem No. 1*. Ah, how furious were those who wanted the South to stay as it was so they could keep fattening on its trouble. How thankful were those who loved this region and wanted it to grow strong again.

A Southwide, unsegregated public meeting was held in the spring of 1938—attended by preachers, writers, union leaders, newspaper editors, churchwomen, plain citizens Negro and white, and Mrs. Franklin D. Roosevelt—to talk about the South's future. Much furor. Name-calling. "The Communists are coming," shrieked the demagogues. (And, of course, two or three did.) Now the demagogues had a new enemy: the liberal, democratic Southerners, whom they immediately labeled "Communists." (It is strange how many Americans will not give democracy or Christianity the least credit for the good things done in our country. Always they credit "the Communists" with our nation's finest acts.) But no one minded the name-calling. It varied things a bit to have a new scapegoat; "the Yankees" had been used so long. There were a thousand white Southerners at that meeting, and they knew they were not Communists. They had gathered with a half-thousand colored Southerners simply to talk things over. They went home, feeling good: they had done it! They had met with Negroes, shared with them their hope for a living, vital, free democracy with no color walls in it.

Now letters, pro and con, began to be written to the press. Careful studies of lynching were published. Essays appeared here, there. More novels about the poor and neglected. Books about sharecropping. More and more unions were organized. People began to accept them as an integral part of a prosperous mature industrial South. The Federal Council of Churches spoke out against race discrimination. The Catholic Church spoke out. In 1942 the first editorial in the South against race segregation appeared in a small magazine. Fact-finding groups popped up here, there, everywhere, North and South. There were more unsegregated meetings. Respect grew for the NAACP—for its Legal Committee was getting results.

Two novels were written—one by a Negro Southerner, one by a white Southerner—which shocked the country into giving grave thought to its human relationships. More novels followed. More race-relations committees, North and South, were formed. More national church groups spoke out. More learned social-science studies appeared; more talk; more quiet thinking and feeling about human rights and human needs.

A few Communists hovered around, of course, during these years, hoping to create an "incident." Their techniques are similar to the demagogue's: they exploit men's best endeavors and men's deepest needs, turning both the good and the bad to their political advantage whenever they can.

But communism had nothing to do with this amazing renascence. In another country, such activity might have been the beginning of revolution. In ours, it was only Americans waking up, changing their minds, correcting mistakes, beginning over again.

We, the people, were shaken by world events, stirred

by spectacular world figures (good and evil): Hitler, Stalin, Chiang Kai-shek, Gandhi, Nehru, Franklin Roosevelt. Aroused from our long sleep, we got busy and began quietly, gradually, to take down the walls that had separated us so long from a full, good, free relationship with our world.

Some, of course, slept through it all. And, after the Second World War ended, many who had once been wide awake and up and doing went back to their secure beds and to sleep.

The public conscience is a drowsy thing. It stirs, and takes another nap; stirs once more, and falls into a deep sleep; is suddenly wide awake and as suddenly stupefied. Racial violence? *Yes, that is wrong,* our conscience said. Discrimination? *No, let me sleep,* our conscience whispered. Gradually it waked up enough to agree, North and South, that "separate but equal" treatment fitted well enough the democratic way. Well enough? *No,* our conscience whispered. For, here, there, the people had begun to realize that man is not animal nor machine; he has a spirit, he has feelings about himself, and this spirit, these feelings cannot be ignored: what hurts his mind or his soul is as important as what hurts his body. Then segregation is wrong? *Wait,* our conscience said sleepily, *wait a little longer.* How long? *Fifty years maybe.*

But some knew we could not wait fifty years. White and colored, North and South, were working together now. And things were done with amazing speed. In less than fifteen years vast changes took place:

The restriction of the poll tax was lifted in many Southern states.

The Supreme Court ruled the white primary unconstitutional, and Negroes in the South were given the vote.

Other Supreme Court rulings on cases brought before it by the NAACP had the result of opening sleeping cars and dining cars to Negroes in the South.

Equalization of opportunity became an accepted principle, after several Supreme Court decisions on test cases brought up by the NAACP, and effected changes that greatly lessened discrimination.

Many Southern universities and state colleges opened their doors to Negroes—without trouble among the students.

Restrictive covenants were ruled by the Supreme Court to be unconstitutional.

Many church schools, especially the Catholic ones, began to accept students of both races.

Numerous professional societies and fraternities, North and South, lifted their racial and religious "gentlemen's agreements."

Many national organizations became unsegregated.

Civil rights laws in a few Northern states began to break down the extra-legal restrictions.

Television and radio programs began to have more white and colored entertainers on the same program, more forums composed of white and colored leaders; commentators began to speak out clearly for human rights.

Negro baseball players were accepted and successful in the major leagues, which not only broke down old fears but created new and friendly identifications in millions of minds. Actors Equity did a good job of "desegregating" the theater.

Restaurants and hotels in Washington, D. C., became unsegregated in 1953.

And, perhaps more significant than all else, the United States Armed Services completed their full integration program in 1954. It was thorough, including the elementary schools on Southern posts, and recreational facilities; and it was harmoniously achieved.

Old walls were crumbling inside and outside us. Not much would be needed to bring them easily, quietly, to the ground.

And, on May 17, 1954, it happened. The Supreme Court's decision about the public schools left no place from this time on for any form of legal segregation in our nation.

It did not come a day too soon. The world alarm clock was ringing. . . .

Now is the time, it was warning us, to take out of the demagogues' hands forever a weapon too dangerous for this atomic age.

Only by ridding ourselves of color walls now, it was warning us, can we rid the world of dictatorship. For every demagogue and every would-be dictator—in America, Russia, Asia, and Africa—is building his power, today, by keeping these two words *color* and *communism* close together. The two are moving in a lock step across the earth, pushing freedom into a smaller and smaller space, crowding the human being hard.

❖ 7 ❖

LET US now leave the American people and look toward the East.

As we watch the Communist conspiracy move steadily across Asia, as we see millions reach out for this new tyranny, we ask ourselves two questions:

What is there in communism that appeals to Asians? What is there in democracy that does not?

The answer is not simple. It lies, however, in large part in two words: *poverty* and *color*.

No American who has not seen it can grasp the extent and acuteness of the poverty of these billion people of Asia—after two hundred years of colonialism. We have known poverty; after the Civil War and until the New Deal, Southerners especially knew it well; other regions have known it also; and there is no city in our country that is not, even now, splotched with it. But we have never, in any part of our nation at any time, experienced the extreme deprivation which is a common thing in Asia. Asia's is zero poverty; ours has rarely dropped below freezing point. Only a small percentage of our people are now touched by it; in Asia almost everybody is affected, and has been, for a long, long time.

The colonial powers who invaded these countries—seeking, not a place (as in Australia, New Zealand, the Americas) for their people to settle, but wealth and, later, a new political strength—did not bring this poverty to the Asians but by their deliberate exploitation of people and resources they increased it. They did not bring ignorance either but they failed in two centuries to alleviate it to an appreciable degree. They did not bring disease but they did nothing to decrease the malaria, cholera, typhus, smallpox they found there. They had no means of doing so for a long time—for medical science had not advanced enough in knowledge or in techniques. But later, when the age of public health and sanitation had come to Europe and America, the colonial powers did not attempt to clean up Asia's streets and provide safe drinking water and sewage systems; nor to eradicate malaria, smallpox, etc. Instead, they segregated their own colonials in neat, clean, antiseptic compounds hoping thus to keep them well and safe. As for the millions around them? Even now, the old Asia "hands" will shrug and say, "Life is cheap in the East."

These health needs, the poverty, the ignorance, are all tied up with Asia's land problems, which were also there when the European powers entered these countries. And they were acute. But colonialism worsened them by strengthening the power of home-grown landlords and the local moneylenders; and by sustaining (as in India) old customs of inheritance which divided and redivided plots of land, generation after generation, until finally families were being supported on one acre or less. When industry came to the West and matured into a way of life, the colonial powers did not industrialize their colonies, whose people needed so desperately to get off the land and into factories where they could make a living wage. Instead, they deliberately restrained industrial growth—wanting to hold these markets for their own manufactured goods.

This colonialism (which in the Asian mind is "democratic colonialism") not only failed to help the people solve their material and physical problems, it did something worse: it deeply humiliated them. For the white colonial was often an arrogant man. Even at his best, he was quietly patronizing, subtly superior—using his white color like a flag in crises small and large, hoisting it above these proud peoples, blandly disregarding their ancient cultures, or, more likely, unaware of the vast and magnificent contributions they had made in the past to world civilization.

A decent chap, perhaps, at home—easy, sportsmanlike, sensitive to the rights of others, concerned for their welfare—he threw his weight around in Asia and Africa. He was a sahib; he felt big, big; he assumed toward "the natives" manners which his fellow-townsmen back in Holland, England, or France would not have tolerated five minutes.

This white colonial forgot that *people have feelings*. He forgot the most important truth about human beings: that no matter how desperately they may need food and shelter and jobs, they hunger more for the esteem and acceptance of their fellow men.

Nearly two hundred years of this white patronage and the economic exploitation that went with it have left Asians with bleeding memories.

It is hard when you have been hurt deeply and for a long time (whether by your family, by other groups, or by other nations) to remember the good things your "persecutors" have done. It requires an honest mind to hold on to the shining exceptions.

There were exceptions and some of the Asian leaders have not forgot. Great Britain (after pressures were exerted) set up in India many good practices; and when India was finally given her independence, it was done with grace and tact by the British. In the French colonies color has never been stressed as it has been in the colonies of the Netherlands and Great Britain. In all these colonies there were many colonial civil servants who were deeply interested in the welfare of the people they worked among and who felt genuine good will toward them. There were the brave and, now and then, imaginative missionaries from many nations (including our own) who did much to alleviate ignorance and suffering; setting up (especially in China) hospitals, medical centers, agricultural experiment stations, excellent schools and colleges.

There are always good human beings in the most oppressive régimes—and times. And these individuals were sprinkled throughout every colonial country—not only great souls like Stanley Jones and Albert Schweitzer, but nameless others who were also selfless and sacrificing. Their work and their lives, and the friendships they formed with the people, are not forgotten by Asians or Africans. This is one of the good bonds that tie us together, today.

But, despite these exceptions and the constructive achievements which took place, Asians and Africans suffered a shame and humiliation and injury whose depths Americans—even Negro Americans—have not known.

Our Civil War hurt; it devastated us physically and spiritually; our Reconstruction left its mark on every mind and heart; the pattern of compulsory segregation in the Southern states that followed has twisted every life, North and South. We have our list of grievances here in the United States against one another, colored against white, South against North.

But colonialism's calendar of sins extends two hundred years through the memories of Asians and Africans. Talk to them, and they will begin to tell you:

- Of Amritsar, in 1919. India had sent a million soldiers to fight in the First World War for a democracy she had never been given a taste of. During a demonstration, in protest at Great Britain's refusal to give rights which the Indians felt they deserved, General Dyer ordered the British soldiers to fire on the protesting thousands—with the result that hundreds were killed and more than twelve hundred wounded.
- Of the shocking "missionary pledge" in 1939, which compelled American missionaries to promise that they would not, while in India, speak out for India's independence.
- Of brusque signs over parks, signs over doors in China, Indochina, India, Indonesia, South Africa, West Africa —wherever white nations have colonized the dark peoples.
- Of clubs and swimming pools reserved *For Europeans Only*.
- Of "passes" (as in South Africa) required of "the natives" as they move back and forth through their everyday life, in their own country.

Of the frequent imprisonment, during the struggle for independence, of hundreds of India's leaders, including Nehru, Madame Pandit, Dhebar, and, of course, Gandhi, many times.

Of the treatment given the Eurasians, Anglo-Indians—results of the white race's back-yard puritanism.

Of the divide-and-weaken policies of every colonizing power.

These are a few of their hurt memories. There are more: thousands of incidents, endless stories of humiliation and deprivation, and segregation.

It is these memories which the Communist demagogues are exploiting today in Asia. We have only to recall the quick success of Southern demagoguery, which built its power on the people's ignorance and insecurity and anxiety, to understand why Communist demagoguery (working on the other side of the color line) is, today, finding the use of exactly the same methods so profitable in Asia.

But demagoguery never succeeds—as Senator Huey Long knew and Senator Joseph McCarthy knows today—by simply arousing painful memories and fears. Demagoguery must offer a danger, yes; but it must also offer a defense against that danger. It must, after arousing the people to a point of hysteria, say, "Now leave it to me. I will take care of all your troubles."

When the Communists enter a country, they begin at once to take care of the people's troubles. They do it in a cheating, spurious way—which is the way of demagoguery, whether of the Communist or democratic variety—but they *do something*.

They are cleaning up the Asian countries they invade—at least, the main streets. They are getting rid of a few of the worst diseases. They are building great dams. They are solving a few of the land problems. They are accumulating a little capital. They are doing these good things by slave labor, by police methods, by forced savings, by a callous and widespread disregard for human life and family relationships. Even so, despite the oppression, these activities give the people a sense of relief and hope. Something is at last being done, they think.

The Communists are also giving the people a valuable present, one that money cannot buy: they tell these Asians, who have been punished by the word *color* so long, that color does not matter any more. Unlike "white democracy," they tell them, communism is not "white communism"; it is "for all the people."

They give them something else: a purpose, a sense of belonging to a vast project whose success depends upon *them*.

Who has ever noticed the people of Asia before? They were mere "coolies" and "peasants." Now it is like belonging to an important club—or perhaps more analogous to the lonely teen-ager's gang. They will take and give a lot of blows for this privilege.

One has only to remember the coolies on Shanghai's streets, a few years ago, to realize the deep sense of exaltation that this *belonging to something important* gives to these anonymous millions.

The Communists have finally learned the demagogic technique of seduction.

In Europe, Communist dictators raped the countries they entered; there was not much sweet talk; their armed forces and secret police moved in and took over and closed the door.

In Asia, their methods are smoother, more gallant. They realize there is not, in many countries, much of a government to take over. It is the people they must deal with, millions of them, and people must be won.

They know, now, the techniques: a good demagogue does not clamp a chain on the people; he persuades them to put it on themselves. He does not set up a secret police to hound you (not at first); he reminds you that to show your loyalty to him you must suspect your neighbor, even your family; you must set yourself up as a secret police. He does not put you on trial; he persuades you to put others on trial; he lets you pass judgment on the loyalty of everybody but yourself, and lets others pass judgment on you.

These standard techniques—used by leaders of gangs, teen-age and political—have for a long time worked well on human beings who are deprived of the recognition they need. They work well with many Asian people today. A few blandishments, a few promises, a few spurious rights, an enemy (the United States will do) on whom they can turn their old resentments, a few real measures of relief—and the Communists have the people with them, even those who want self-determination and independence.

Then something begins to happen. Something that cannot happen in our country as long as we uphold our Constitution and respect our Supreme Court and cling to our Bill of Rights. But it can happen in Asia: the demagogues turn overnight into dictators. With the inner logic of a nightmare, the chains begin to tighten; the secret police appear; the new rights begin to shrivel—and the new importance; there is in this nightmare no protest—your mouth may open but no sound comes out; there is no way to protect one's self from this monster who has suddenly lost his smile. The people are trapped. It is true: "color does not matter any more"; but freedom does not matter either, nor one's rights, nor one's friends and family, nor one's own life.

And yet, though they feel the pressures tightening, they still have hope. In a few years, they say, things will be better. A few years do not seem long to wait to patient millions who have waited centuries without hope.

"But why is there so much distrust of us?" Americans ask. "*We* have never colonized the peoples of Asia and Africa. Only once for a brief time we controlled the Philippines. But we gave them independence, and now our relationship is warm and friendly. We too were once a colony; we know what it feels like. We want Asians to be free. We are on their side."

It is true; we have not colonized any country of Asia or Africa, although we have profited from the colonizing activities of other powers. We enjoyed the privileges of extraterritoriality in China, and have often enjoyed special privileges in other Asian countries simply because we are white. And there have been times when Americans in Asia have pretended they too were sahibs, exhibiting a superior attitude which did our country no good. The United States' role in colonialism has been somewhat analogous to the North's role in American segregation: a matter, largely, of too many gentlemen's agreements and too much silent acquiescence. This is well known to Asians and Africans. We have supported colonial powers and their puppets when we should have been supporting democratic leaders of the people. This official vacillation of ours has again and again caused the Asian and African people's faith in our democratic integrity to be shaken. And there are the McCarran-Walters immigration restrictions, which have deepened resentments, everywhere.

But, for the most part, our record is clean.

Then why do the countries of Asia distrust the United States so much? Why are the Indian leaders, the Indochinese leaders, the African leaders, and others and still others, so afraid of our motives?

Once more, the answer lies in two words: *color* and *power*.

As long as we have legal segregation inside the United States we are a "white democracy" to the Asians and the Africans. They may like individuals among us; they may admire certain of our excellent qualities (and they do); they may, and do, appreciate our generosity (which is, perhaps, not too impressive when one considers our great resources); but *as long as we practice segregation against colored people, as long as there are signs over doors in this land, as long as there are laws in any of the states making race segregation compulsory, as long as our officials (whom we, the people, have chosen) make insulting public statements about the darker people,* Asians and Africans will not trust us.

They have had enough of "white democracy." They are, to put it bluntly, fed up.

Communist colonialism may prove to be ten times worse than the brand of colonialism they have experienced for two centuries, but at least it is something different. And in their hearts, no matter how informed their minds are, they cannot believe it is a menace to them—as long as the Communists do not segregate people who are colored. Yes, the Communists may be discriminating against the Jews in Russia (as the world has recently heard); there may be the millions of political deviationists in slave camps that Russian refugees say are there; but in Asia "they don't discriminate against Asians or the so-called colored. And never will they do it, because they need us as their friends."

This is what millions of Asians feel. It may not often be said plainly around conference tables. Officials may shy off from so painful a subject. But the people's humiliation runs deep—deep enough perhaps to cause them to use bad judgment in the decisions that they are now making for their countries. They are making these decisions; no leader can drive them where they do not want to go.

But more is involved than Asia's hurt memories, and its urgent economic needs.

The United States is the most powerful nation on earth. The Asians fear power. They have felt its great weight on them before. They do not want to be pressured into doing anything. They want to make their own decisions. They want Asia for the Asians—not in the chauvinistic meaning of Japan's old slogan, but with intentions more analogous to those of our own Monroe Doctrine. They want, above all else, to be independent, self-determining nations, and they want to work out the achieving of this goal "by themselves." Perhaps that is not possible in the age we now live in; but it is what they want. If they live, they want to live in their own way; if they die—"at least" (they whisper) "let us die in our own way."

And they fear that we will not let them do so. They dread the terrible power of the hydrogen bomb. They resent the fact that this monstrous evil is in white hands. They remember that the United States used the atom bomb against Asians. Who in Asia can ever forget! They are not at all certain that we would not use the hydrogen bomb against them, too, if we felt it necessary to stop our enemies. Do we not experiment with it in Asian waters?

But Russia too has the hydrogen bomb. Yes, Russia has it; but Asians do not believe Russia will ever use it against *them*. She will use it against "capitalistic, white nations," many Asians will tell you. They believe this. And this belief is grounded on their deep feelings, their most hurting memories, but also on the careful appraisal they have made of the American-Russian conflict.

This begins to pull us into what feels like a very small

room with no exit. But actually there are many doors we can open. There is much that we can do to change what is not a situation but a state of mind.

There is no situation in the world today that is too difficult to solve. If we could only believe it! Our difficulties, East and West, lie in our state of mind—made inflexible and stiff from fears and memories.

What we need above all else is to change that state of mind.

Why do we not begin at the easiest place—here at home? Why not do the simplest thing? To give up color segregation, to do it quickly and harmoniously, is a small price to pay. It will cost no American lives. No great sum of money needs to be expended; indeed, money will be saved, for the dual system of life in the Southern states is an exorbitant drain on local and national economy.

But in the doing of it, the world's knotted state of mind will ease. Other strands will begin to loosen. Suspicion of the United States will diminish. Trust in American integrity will increase. Faith in our moral strength will return to us, too. As the old guilts grow small, hope will grow large. We shall not fear the Communist conspiracy so desperately because we shall be in a stronger moral position to combat it. It will become for us a rational danger—not the terror it now is in many minds.

Were this to happen, were such a reasonable, hopeful state of mind brought about by our willingness, as a great and powerful nation, to *act first* in this world-sized dilemma of color, generous feelings would be released in millions of people across the earth—people who are not Communist, who do not want this new and terrible form of tyranny, but who have turned away from a democracy that has again and again sacrificed its prestige for white prestige.

Just here, we might wisely remind ourselves—and the world—that our government has never imposed segregation on colored people. We, the people, did so; we rubbed the shine off that great word *democracy;* and it is we who must put it back again. When we do so, it will not be governments but the people of the world who will respond to our act.

This may seem too simple a solution; but the point is, it is not a solution at all: it is a beginning. People are feeling creatures who respond to the decent, honest acts of other people. They cannot witness this change in our way of life without feeling lifted up by it. They have thought of us so long as powerful and wealthy and, from their point of view, arrogant in our overesteem of whiteness. They see us, in their minds, surrounded by atomic weapons, heavily industrialized, threatening. Only humility is fitting for a nation with so much power and strength; and this act of giving up a long-time segregation would seem to the world a humble acknowledgment of a mistake made and now righted.

If we could only recognize the age we are living in! An age in which permanent segregation has no place. For this is an age of no walls between the people of the earth: no kind of segregation, no kind of iron curtains. It is the age of wholeness, of acceptance of every man, every woman, every child as a human being. It is an age of concern for human suffering. There was a time when we felt compelled to hide the world's misery from ourselves. We can feel this concern now because we can *do something about it*. People care about one another; about the stranger whose name they do not know. Children and their feelings have become important—even to the heads of governments—for we know that how children think about themselves, what they feel, what they learn to cherish, will determine our human future.

One world ... one future. There is no escaping it. And who wants to? For the choice is ours as to whether we keep that future free and open for growth. We can do so, if we wish. We need not let it become the massive tyranny that the Communist conspiracy would make it.

It is worth working for: that future. Worth a bit of inconvenience, worth the pain of changing our minds, worth the sloughing off of ignorance.

Men have dreamed, for thousands of years, of a time when all people would be accepted as persons; when human differences would be treasured; when men would be free and, at the same time, responsible; when the great chasms of ignorance and fear and distance and poverty would be filled up. That age has now come. We have all we need to make it a reality for the earth's people.

And we, as the strongest nation on earth, should begin to live in it. We should lead the way. If we do, perhaps Russia too will realize that there is no place in this age for the archaic tyranny and slavery she is attempting to impose on the world—a tyranny made worse than any the ancient world witnessed because of the modern techniques and machinery that can enforce it so massively. Perhaps the young Asian and African nations, profoundly experienced as people but inexperienced as nations, can avoid the backward steps which we, as a young nation a hundred and fifty years ago, did not avoid; and which Russia, in the different context of our modern age, has not avoided either. Such a return to the past is not only too dangerous, it is completely unnecessary.

But how can we Americans say such a thing when we still cling to color segregation?

The emotional deadlock must somehow be broken. And we can break it.

There are so many things we can do, and say. Little things, big things; that will ease hearts and minds, that will open doors, that will lift our spirits. Vision will come to us as we do them; imaginations will be stirred. Our ordeal will be transformed into a great creative venture. We shall have started on our way toward assuming real leadership in bringing our world into a harmonious whole, where no nation dominates but all work together freely; where each maintains its integrity and cherishes its unique ways, but all share in the common tasks of lifting the earth's people to a level where they can live decently and feel that they are, at last, members of the human family and will, from this time on, share equally in its future.

Will we do it? It depends on you and me.

II

There Are Things to Do and Things to Say

THE GIVING UP of segregation is a change that takes place in minds. It will affect our external way of life very little.

We are confronted with no loss of life, no rationing of food and fuel, as in war; no economic difficulties, as in a depression; no risk of crippling effects, as in certain epidemics; no loss of property or disruption of communication, as in storms. What we are facing today is the crumbling of an old idea.

Briefly, this strange idea clung to by the white group for nearly two centuries is this: "People who are white are superior to other people. Because they are, they have the right to dominate human beings with darker skins: to set them apart, to tell them where they may go, to give them fixed places in buses, to keep them out of certain jobs, certain public schools, certain parts of town, and certain public buildings. The white group, simply because it is white, can decide which of his constitutional rights the colored citizen may have, and when he may have them."

Along with this idea goes a threat. The threat is turned

toward white people: "If there are white people who think it wrong to take another person's rights away from him, if there are those who feel that segregation contradicts their religious beliefs, they must conform, even so; for should the walls between white and colored come down, a terrible disaster would follow."

Set down in words, the idea and its threat are preposterous. In the dark interiors of minds, where words are not put into sentences, perhaps it is possible to cling to it. Lifted out into the light of reason and knowledge and our concern for each other, it makes no sense at all. The whole thing dissolves, like a bad dream. Who, in our modern world, could believe it!

And yet there are people who do. Intelligent, well-intentioned people who were taught this idea in childhood by loved ones and who were shaken by its dire threat; ignorant people who have never heard anything else. It seeped into them before they knew words: became a way of thinking and feeling. As they grew older, they learned it again, on the street, in school, in segregated church, as they read their newspapers, as they walked through doors marked *White* and avoided doors marked *Colored*. Such lessons go deep down in the mind.

In the South, in the border states, millions of us were taught these lessons. But some of us have changed our minds. We know now the threat is an old ghost story. We can smile at it. We have seen that nothing bad happens when white and colored people go to universities together; nothing dreadful occurs when they work in the same union or worship in the same church or go into the same restaurant. World events, books, plays, forums, radio, television, sports, travel, have taught us new lessons about human behavior, and we believe them.

We have learned, too, the difference between public and private life. We know, now, that American public life belongs to everybody. One's private life is one's own. Every citizen's right to both is protected by our Constitution. Each of us has the right—given us by our government when we were born—to move freely through the common public life, to share equally in its opportunities, to be protected equally by the law. Each of us also has the right never to be intruded upon in home or club, or interfered with in our personal relationships. These matters are now clear in the minds of millions who were reared in strict segregation. They understand.

But there are millions who do not yet understand. These cling to the right to tell Negroes what they can do; they hold fast to the idea of white superiority, to the belief in segregation. They cannot bear to give up the old way. It has become a crutch on which they lean. It fills deep psychic needs, different for different personalities. To some, "the Negro" is a scapegoat on whom they can freely vent their hate; to some, the "race problem" gives a respectable name to anxieties they long to express; to others, white superiority offers prestige, power, money, which they would not otherwise have; to a few, darkness and dark people have become equated with the forbidden and mysterious part of their natures, and they need walls to shut this evil away.

But most white people, while enjoying the unearned

privileges their whiteness gives them, do not depend on these privileges nor need walls to prop their personalities against. Change upsets them simply because they do not know how many will change with them. They are comfortable only when they do what others do. If millions give up segregation quickly, they too will give it up.

There is, of course, no solid white opinion in the United States, and no solid South. People, white and colored, vary in numberless ways in the intensity of their feelings about segregation.

But there is one feeling which most share: anxiety. They do not know how integration will work out. They are, suddenly, fearing the old threat they heard in childhood. "Bad things will happen," they were told ten thousand times. What bad things? No one quite knows. To put this dread into words is difficult. But many feel that if they don't observe segregation (whether they like it or not) they will be punished, somehow, by somebody. If it is possible to delay the change, they must do so.

This is the mood, this smoldering dread, on which the demagogue throws his inflammatory words. Suddenly it blazes into panic.

We saw it happen, in the autumn of 1954, in a small Delaware town. The board of education made the decision to send a few Negro students to the white high school. There was tension, yes—a little insecurity, a few mutterings, but nothing that could not have become harmonized in a few days. For most Americans are decent people; most would like to do the right thing. Then, suddenly, an agitator came to town, an opportunist who seized this chance to fatten himself on the people's fears. He began to talk big and loud about "the white man's rights," about "trouble brewing," about "invasion of the home," and "socializing" and all the rest of it. A few people's anxiety turned to terror. Terror is contagious: others became disturbed. Strikers paraded the streets. There was anger, there were threats. The Negro students were temporarily withdrawn from the school. The mob, not the law of our land, won the first round.

The panic spread to Baltimore and Washington, where a harmonious integration was taking place. There were more tension, more strikers, many withdrawals of children from schools. But the mob did not win in these two cities, for the leadership was strong and mature, and quickly harmony and order were restored.

How did these leaders do it?

By their silence? No. The future is not stumbled upon; it is created out of words and acts. Good leaders know this. Even before the Supreme Court's decision they had begun to prepare their cities for the change. Editorials and newspaper stories reminded the people of important things: that our democracy is based on the Constitution; that its strength lies in the people's regard for its laws; that disesteem for the Constitution, a cheapening of respect for law, would precipitate not only a vast delinquency among the young but would endanger the foundations of our government. Segregation may give a few white people a feeling of psychic protection; but every one of us is protected by the Constitution and the Supreme Court which interprets it. This constitutional protection is real and powerful, and none of us can do without it; the other is a fantasy made up in uneasy minds.

When the school trouble came, the leaders calmly, and with sympathy for the anxious ones, spoke plainly, each in his own way and in his own vocabulary. In editorials, sermons, on radio, television, in conferences with parents and with pupils, the values we cherish as free people were brought out and looked at; the problems, real and unreal, were discussed. Teachers did much; the boards of education acted wisely; the police force were quietly firm in their insistence on obedience to the law.

Because of this intelligent leadership external order was restored.

But something more creative happened: people grew. Leaders grew, also. Values shifted. Inside many minds, first things were put first. New questions were asked about the meaning of the public school in a democracy, about the growth of children. What role do esteem and acceptance play in a child's life? How do his feelings affect his capacity to learn, his values, his image of himself? What can the school do to help a child relate himself to his human world? How can it help him live in *his* age—not the age of his parents and grandparents?

The questions would not be answered at once; but the asking of them is important.

There is no doubt about it: if Baltimore and Washington succeed in bringing white and colored school children together, if these children learn to live in peace with one another, Baltimore and Washington will be better cities. They will have achieved a measure of greatness they had not known before. Their vision will be larger; their skill in working out difficult human problems will have grown; their knowledge of children will be more profound; and the community itself will be more mature.

They will have mastered their ordeal. And, in doing it, they will open up new potentialities for all the people.

While this was happening in the two big Southern cities which have the largest proportion of colored to white school children in our nation, the rest of the country was not looking on complacently. A spirit of sympathy, of common concern was growing; a conviction was crystallizing that integration of our schools, like public health, is not a matter for politicians to dabble in or exploit to their personal advantage. They have no right here. This problem concerns children and their future. It is a task that challenges the best minds of our nation, that needs skilled techniques, and all the knowledge the experts have gathered up about human relationships.

At the same time, because it touches every one of us, there can be no innocent bystanders. We are all involved.

The good thing, the encouraging thing, is that we can help. There are things we can say and things we can do.

Some of these things are so simple the most timid and cautious among us can safely do them. Other tasks require skill, resourcefulness—and perhaps more daring than many wish to assume. No matter: do the things that are easy for you to do. They count in building a mood of good will in your community; they reduce tension in your own mind; they encourage others to act creatively.

The Simple, Undramatic Things We Can All Do:

1. Use courtesy titles when you speak to Negroes or about them, and when you speak to any strange Negro. As the world becomes more civilized, surely we shall accord courtesy titles to all human beings, regardless of the jobs they hold, the wages they make. Southerners can begin now in a small way by using courtesy titles in their speech and by seeing to it that their newspapers use them. In recent years, many Southern newspapers have been doing this; many others, however, do not. The small weekly newspaper and the small city newspaper have been slow to change. Check on your newspaper. Does it use courtesy titles when speaking of Negroes? Does it still use "colored" to set Negroes apart from other Americans? Does it overemphasize crime and violence in its news stories of the colored community? Does it report on the creative and constructive efforts of Negro citizens? If not, suggest to the editor by telephone or letter that these changes be made.

2. In many minds, during the past few years, the stereotype named "the Negro" has disappeared. Taking the place of this one hard image are numberless fluid mem-

ories of actual people as different as Eartha Kitt, Marian Anderson, Mrs. Mary McLeod Bethune, Ann Hedgman, Willie Mays, Dr. Ralph Bunche, Dr. Channing Tobias, Richard Wright.

But people still talk about "the Negro." Why? Because millions of white people have never met an educated Negro and other millions have never met any Negro. Actual contact is of enormous importance in changing mental images.

There are things you can do about this:

(a) When people talk to you about "the Negro," ask them which Negro they are speaking about. When you are told stories that discredit the Negro race, cancel them out by telling the good specific things you know about individual Negroes.

(b) If you have never met a Negro, now is the time to meet a few. If you are Southern and know only the Negroes who have worked for you, arrange to meet a few Negroes in the professions.

(c) If you live in the South, perhaps there is not too distant from your town a Negro college which you can visit. Take your children with you. If you live near a Negro hospital, perhaps you and a group of your friends can visit it.

(d) In the North, through your PTA or with the cooperation of the principal, you can arrange for a Negro doctor or nurse, artist or writer, baseball player or naturalist, to visit your children's school either at assembly or in classroom and discuss his field of work, his special interests.

(e) If your child's school is still segregated, why not plan for a group of students to visit an integrated school to see how it works? The important thing is to break down the old isolation and get together as simple human beings.

One church in a Southern town invited a Negro officer of the Air Force, and his wife, to tell the congregation about integration in the armed services. It is a great success story. More Americans should hear it.

Other churches have invited Negro ministers to preach at morning or evening services.

A group of young people held a forum on rehabilitation of the disabled and invited a Negro doctor to speak.

There are endless possibilities. However small the town, however cautious, speakers of the Negro race can be brought in if sponsored by church or civic groups. It is a small thing to do. Its effect on minds and attitudes will be large.

This coming together *as people* is important for the Negro community, too. Both races tend to stereotype each other. There are many educated Negroes in the South who have never been in a white home and have met white Southerners in only a brief, casual way. Their ideas of white people are, oftentimes, incredibly distorted. Cultural isolation is a soil in which lies and anxiety-fantasies grow unchecked. It is important for understanding between the races that the leaders of the groups know each other. It will not be easy. Many Negroes are sensitive; they have old, hurt memories; they are reluctant to be with white people.

THERE ARE THINGS TO DO AND THINGS TO SAY 85

You can help here.

(f) If you are colored, invite a few white women to visit your PTA. Show them your school; introduce the teachers to them. If you are white, invite a few Negro women to visit your PTA; introduce them to your teachers. Invite one of them to speak to your club, not on race relations but on a common interest: gardening, current novels, or teen-age delinquency. If you live in a city, you have rich resources in the Negro community to draw upon. In the small towns, unfortunately, many of the women of the Negro race are compelled to work too hard to have much time for books. It might be a significant experience, however, to ask one of these mothers to talk to your group of the problems of caring for their small children when they are in domestic service; or the recreational problems their teen-age girls and boys have in an isolated community.

(g) Bring together a small group from both races to discuss the town's common problem of integration of schools. One meeting will not accomplish much. Ten meetings will be most effective in changing the climate of opinion in the community. An interesting project would be to study the methods used in schools that have recently completed a successful integration (such as Claymont, Delaware; Phoenix, Arizona).

(h) The Chamber of Commerce and other civic clubs can do much to break down fears and old stereotypes. They can have Negro speakers at luncheons; they can bring together groups of white and Negro citizens to talk things over; they can invite an expert in the field of education to outline concrete ways of making the transition from the old to the new; they can have someone who is well informed speak about the Communists' use of the race issue as a means of destroying the Asians' confidence in the United States. This turning from the past and looking straight at the future is the way tensions are eased. Once hope and good will are established, the problems shrink in size.

The federal government can help by setting up an emergency fund (which it undoubtedly will) to aid communities in making the transition. This, surely, is a situation which will strain financial resources of many small towns—not only because new schools must be built quickly but because, in order to achieve a harmonious transition, much adult education must be carried on. Teachers and supervisors will need special training. Every community should send a group of its leaders to visit an integrated school. Every community should have resources of books, films, factual studies of how integration is being carried out elsewhere. These things cost money. Many of the techniques and communication resources developed by the United States Public Health Service could be wisely used in this emergency situation.

3. Write letters to the press suggesting measures that will help bring about a harmonious change. A letter should open doors, not slam them. When we feel crowded together by an event, a stress, we want exits; we do not want to hear keys turning in locks.

Letters to a firm or institution about a specific situation

are often effective. The letters should be courteous and sympathetic. You are not passing judgment: you are making suggestions; you hope the reader of the letter will accept your suggestions. Tact will help him do so.

(a) Write to stores that show discrimination toward Negro patrons. (Many still do, North and South.) Suggest ways by which the personnel's attitude might be changed.

Twenty letters may change an unfair racial policy. They did so, not long ago, in a department store in a Southern city. There were signs over drinking fountains. Twenty white customers, each of whom had a charge account at the store, wrote the manager and suggested that the signs be removed. It would be good for business, they said, and good for the feelings of the community. Not one letter scolded or indulged in name-calling. Each stated briefly and courteously the advantages that would come from the sign's removal. The signs were down in less than two weeks.

(b) Write to hospitals about the signs over drinking fountains. Suggest that these white-supremacy mottos do not make for better health—either physical or mental.

(c) Write to your local board of education, and to your governor. Say that you, personally, are ready for integration, that you believe it will work if the community is prepared in advance for it. Take your stand now.

(d) Write your minister, or speak to him about the moral issues involved in segregation. Urge him to speak out plainly for obedience to our laws. Ask him to preach a sermon on the spiritual harm which legal segregation inflicts on every child. If he does so, praise him. Express your pleasure to the board of trustees who hold it in their power to dismiss him.

Letters of praise are important. They give courage; they ease the loneliness one feels when taking an unpopular stand.

4. This is a time to read. Sensitive, honest autobiographies have been written by Negroes, white Southerners, South Africans, and Asians. Many novels, in recent years, have been concerned with this worldwide problem of color. There are the scholarly books for serious students. There is one excellent account of integration in the armed services. There are numerous books on Asia, Africa.

(a) Ask your public library to set up a shelf of these books.

(b) Urge your bookstore to keep them in stock.

(c) Suggest to your club that a few of these books be reviewed.

(d) Suggest to the book editor of your newspaper that he list ten or fifteen helpful books. (There is a list on pages 121-26 of this book.)

5. (a) Suggest to your local radio or television station topics for round-table discussion. A few possible ones are:

The role of the public school in a democracy.
The psychological effects of legal segregation on colored and white children.
How to prepare the community for a harmonious acceptance of integrated public schools.

Is the people's ordeal (whether it be epidemic, flood, or sudden change in social patterns) a legitimate area for exploitation by politicians?

(b) An interesting program might be built around the idea of individuals quietly talking together about past experiences. Two Southerners—one white, one colored—might tell of their childhoods: the fun they had as youngsters; what they liked to eat; the ideas they had about the other race; the racial incidents that troubled them when they were children. This honest, simple sharing of old memories would be a moving experience for a television audience. A profound identification would take place in the minds of the listeners; many would realize, perhaps for the first time, how much in common white and colored Southerners have and how deeply we cherish these common experiences.

(c) To bring children of both races together on television programs would have creative results for them and for their audience.

(d) Mothers from the two races might discuss the comic-book problem, or children's programs on radio and television, or the recreational needs of the community.

For decades, false fears about race, false problems, have cluttered our minds. It would be refreshing for actual people of both races to discuss together concrete problems and their common interests.

6. There are troublemakers in both groups: the tactless ones, the cynics, the gossips, the bullies, the pushers. Wherever they are, and regardless of color or sex, they

are highly inflammable material and should be treated as such.

If you were to meet on the highway a truck marked EXPLOSIVES you would give it a wide berth. Do the same with these explosive personalities. Don't let them provoke you to anger. Think of them as unstable personalities, as unhappy individuals who have not found a constructive way to use up their hate feelings. Don't think of them as "the Negro" or "the white race." Keep in mind that we too may be a bit unstable; we too may not find it easy always to move along calmly under stress: we may, perhaps, read evil intentions into innocent or careless acts because of our own guilt feelings. This is a time when it is wise for us to allow one another a wide margin of error.

7. There are things to say—and things we should not say.

For a long time white people have defended the indefensible. In doing it, we have cluttered our minds with shabby excuses, old superstitions, false fears, and a few whopping lies. To get out in the clear where we can see what the actual difficulties are, we need to do a bit of mental housecleaning. A way to begin is to discard the old habits of speech and spurious arguments used too long.

Don't use depreciating words like "nigger," "darkie," "coon."
Don't tell race jokes that discredit Negroes or whites, or any other group under pressure.

Don't repeat rumors of violence and of plans for violence. Rumors throw gasoline on a smoldering fire. If you fear violence is brewing, go to the leaders of your community who can do something about it. Tell them, not your neighbor.

Don't use the old excuse of "filth and smells." It is poverty and ignorance and lack of hope, not skin color, that bring uncleanliness. Body odors are more often determined by emotional strain or ill health than by filth. The more acute odors are usually those caused by glandular disorders. White people have these difficulties too. Why, otherwise, would magazines with a white circulation carry the B.O. ads?

Don't say, "Segregation cannot be done away with overnight." It is a silly statement. A house is not built overnight but it is built, often, in six months. A sick person may not get well overnight, but he may have recovered within a week or two. Integration is a creative job, a process that will take effort, imagination, faith. To do the job well may require many communities a year or two; others may effect the change-over in a few months. In backward rural regions it may require four or five years, even with federal financial aid. The length of time depends on the community's leadership, on its people's intelligence, resources, desire, and moral stamina. If a community lacks these qualities, it may take a dangerously long time. If it has them, the change will come quickly.

Don't say, "It will take fifty years." Such a statement encourages people to disobey the law. It does more: it breeds unconcern for the children who are suffering from the evils of segregation. In fifty years two more generations of children will be twisted and misshapen. Can we afford so vast a human loss?

Don't get into heated arguments. Listen to the other person's point of view; it may not be valid but he has a need for believing it is. And this need we can respect. Tact and honesty together are priceless; separated, both lose in effectiveness.

Don't talk about "the white man's rights." No white man, no Negro, has any right because of his color. Whatever moral rights he has are his because he belongs to the human family. Whatever legal rights he has in our country are his because they are guaranteed by our Constitution to everybody, regardless of race, creed, or sex.

Sometimes we become confused and claim rights that are not ours. A citizen in our country has the right to send his children to the public schools; he does not have the right to decide who their schoolmates will be. He has the right to live wherever he wishes; he does not have the right to determine who shall live next to him. He has the right to work, but he does not have the right to choose his fellow workers. He has the right to attend a theater or public entertainment; he cannot dictate to the box office who will sit in the next seat.

Don't write a letter to the press stating what "the South wants." State only what *you* want. There is no Southerner who can speak for the South. There are about thirty-two million white people in the South, many of whom have come from other regions. There are about ten million Negroes in the South. Each of these forty-two million people has his own opinion. And there are numberless shades of opinion—ranging from the compulsive segregationist (white or colored) who would go to any length to keep the defenses he has grown used to, to the mature human being who accepts himself as one member of the human family, who cherishes his rights but knows the same laws protecting him are protecting other citizens also.

Don't talk about "undue hardship" for white people in giving up segregation. It is a graceless thing to say. If only we who are white could *feel* what Negroes have gone through: the day-by-day, hour-by-hour humiliation which this system of segregation has inflicted on them; the lack of security of body and mind; the poverty and discrimination they have endured. Perhaps this dulling of the white person's imagination and sympathy has been one of the worst consequences of segregation. It has put a third skin on too many minds and hearts.

Don't talk about the "dangers" of giving up legal segregation. "Socializing," "invasion of the home," are anxiety-inducing phrases. That is why demagogues and agitators use them. Regardless of how we may feel about segregation, there is not one responsible person who wants to create more fear in his community.

Instead, why not remind ourselves and others of the harmonious integration that has *already taken place* in the armed services, on dining cars, in universities, hospitals, professional societies, in many churches and schools?

It is time to leave the land of ghosts and come out into the broad daylight, where we can see things *as they are*.

Were legal segregation to be ended today, what would happen tomorrow?

The signs over public doors would be gone. That is all.

Stores would open promptly. Business would be as good as ever. Clubs would meet as usual. Newspapers, radio and television programs would appear on schedule. Communication facilities would be in good order. The banks would open. Unemployment would not increase. You would go to your bridge party and no one would be present except those invited. You would see at school—after the change-over had been effected by the school board—a few children who had not been there before. Just children, not ghosts. They might have darker faces or pinker ones, but they would not be less attractive than the other children. In behavior and intelligence they would measure up to the average.

This is the way it would be.

Whatever upheavals there were would happen *inside people's minds*. Only there.

Now this is good to realize. For each of us can keep his own mind in order. (If we cannot, we need to put ourselves in the care of those who can protect us.) We can maintain serenity within ourselves. And we can ease the strain for others. Our children will be relaxed, if we are. Our friends can be calmed down, often, by a few quiet words. A sense of humor is priceless at a time like this.

The responsibility is ours to keep the doors open by reminding one another of the good things which can come out of this "trouble."

Trouble. . . . Why do we fear it? Why do we dread ordeal? Every good thing the human race has experienced was trouble for somebody. Our birth was trouble for our mothers. To support us was trouble for our fathers. Books, paintings, music, great buildings, good food, ideas, the nameless joys and excitements which add up to what we call "a good life" came out of the travail of countless hearts and minds.

Then why do we not value trouble as the catalytic agent it is? Because we do not want to change. Change shoves us into the new; it makes us hew out a path through an unknown future; it drives us to learn, compels us to stretch our imagination; it whispers, "Let go that old defense; it is no more useful to you now than are bows and arrows to a modern army. Find a new defense —one that fits the age you live in, one that will help you without destroying you."

Stretching hurts; learning hurts; hewing out a new path makes minds and bodies sore. There is never a convenient time to change, to seek the hidden potentialities we possess.

And yet, change is necessary. When it comes, it cannot be brought about successfully and harmoniously unless new defenses, new resources, are found for the old ones lost or destroyed. This is the number one bargain we human beings make with ourselves and our world, with our families and our religions and our political systems, too: *If you take my crutch away, you must give me another or teach me how to walk. If you take away my belief in the importance of skin color,* says the segregationist, *you must give me a new image of the human being I can be proud of and identify with.*

How creative an experience the giving up of segregation will become for our nation depends upon how well we keep this old human bargain with each other.

And this depends on you and me: on the quality of our vision and our ability to use with imagination the magnificent resources, moral and intellectual and material, which we, as a people, possess.

III

The Twenty-five Questions

THESE are the questions that have won elections for politicians in the South and provoked housing incidents in the North. They are slogans which real-estate boards and home owners often use when defending restrictive covenants. They are weapons which no race agitator can do without.

They are troublemakers. Based on a few false assumptions whose roots go deep into old superstitions and folk fears of the past, most of them hold a vague, insistent threat, difficult to put into words, but there.

Everyone has heard them. Most of us have asked at least a few of them. You hear them, today, in Westchester County and in small Georgia towns, in Connecticut and the Mississippi Delta and California; Johannesburg, South Africa, may offer a few variations, but the basic questions are asked there, too; one heard them often in Asia in colonial days, in the white man's clubs; Hitler gave them a sinister twist in *Mein Kampf*, but, stripped of their Teutonic verbiage, they sound much like the words Bilbo once sprinkled throughout his speeches.

No machiavellian brain thought them up. No propaganda committee formulated them. They grew slowly, one by one, out of a deep need to defend the morally indefensible, and flourished on the people's ignorance until they became thick walls in minds, shutting out what many did not want to see.

Most of these questions are dead now, killed off not only by scientific facts and our increasing knowledge of cultures and of the human body and mind, but by world events and a sharpened awareness of men's interdependence. And yet, in spite of a widespread dissemination of facts and news and values, people still use them as arguments against integration.

The Questions and a Few Brief Answers

The questions are formulated here just as they were asked me by two hundred audiences to whom I talked on human relations. Small-town club, university forum, church study group, North, South, and Midwest—the questions were the same. A curious lack of freshness was apparent—as if all the thinking on this topic of color and segregation had become stereotyped. They cluster around a few fuzzy premises which have to do with heredity and "blood" and environment, culture, economics, the Bible, the law and morals, time, and "what Negroes like." The answers given here are brief and simple. More complete answers can be found in the books listed on pages 121-26.

CULTURE

Q. 1. Don't you think each race should keep its culture separate?

A. 1. There is no culture anywhere in the world based solely on race or religion. There are groups of people living in various parts of the earth, each with a culture different in many ways from other cultures. All are phases of the human culture, which extends back to the beginning of man's history. All are indebted to other cultures for much that they now call their own. Negroes and whites in the United States are products of the American culture, which, in turn, is indebted to various European, Asian, American Indian, African, and Caribbean groups for much that is prized highly as "American."

Q. 2. The Negro has done pretty well, considering he has been out of savagery only three hundred years. Don't you think it takes time to civilize people?

A. 2. This question is a favorite with demagogues. Let us take it piecemeal. There is no meaning to the words "the Negro." There are Negroes. Most of the Negroes now in the United States were born here. They were not born *out of* an African culture, they were born *into* our American culture. From the day they were born they began to learn as quickly as do white babies. Culture is not something one inherits: one *learns* it and begins learning it the first weeks of one's life. A child learns what the family teaches him, and, later, what school, church, friends and enemies, books, the street, and television teach him. His experiences and his awareness of their meaning give him, in large part, his quality as a human being.

Q. 3. The rate of violence and lawlessness is much higher among Negroes than whites. Isn't this proof that they are still primitive?

A. 3. It is proof only that under a segregated regime the environment of colored town is not as good for children to grow up in as is the environment of white town. Poverty, lack of schooling facilities, discrimination of a dozen kinds, social rejection, make a poor growing climate for children. Another reason is that the law in the South is not administered with equal justice for Negroes and whites. Negroes can get by with crimes when committed *against Negroes* because law-enforcement officers and courts will often look the other way. This leniency encourages them to take out their violent feelings on one another. But a crime against a white is treated with extreme harshness. (This situation has improved in recent years.) When Negroes share equally in the freedoms of American citizenship they will be willing and able to share equally in the responsibilities.

INTERMARRIAGE AND "BLOOD" AND INHERITANCE

Q. 4. If races mix, will it not result in an inferior breed of people as "mongrelization" does with animals?

A. 4. There are no "pure" races. There are no blood

types that correspond to skin color. There is only one race: the human race. The variations (such as skin color, eye color, height, shape of nose, etc.) in the appearance of groups are due to climate, food, and thousands of years of inbreeding. There are no proofs that white people as a group are superior or inferior to colored people as a group, nor is there proof that children born of mixed marriages are inferior or superior biologically. There are white geniuses and morons, and colored geniuses and morons, and geniuses and morons who are the children of mixed marriages. The differences between individuals of the same group are conspicuous. The differences between groups are relatively superficial and almost wholly those of environment.

But of this we are certain: the human race is profoundly different from animals, because of what we call "human culture." What is good or bad for a horse or dog is not necessarily good or bad for a man. We became human (1) because we learned to talk and share with each other what we had learned and we can do this regardless of differences in skin color; and (2) because, in our prolonged infancy, we were given tenderness and care, and learned the survival value of concern for others. As Dr. Lawrence Kubie reminds us, every human child is a premature baby in the sense that at birth he is completely helpless. All he can do for himself is breathe. He *learns from others.* And he does so, in large part, because of human speech. Yet he is not born knowing his mother's language. He learns it. The physical differences of various groups are no more conspicuous than are language differences. Yet any child on earth capable of speech can learn, if he begins early enough, any language spoken anywhere.

By means of his ability to communicate with others and the race's skill in recording knowledge, the human being is able to learn and make use of the dreams and ideas and discoveries of strangers whatever their color, who lived thousands of years ago, or yesterday; and, in turn, to teach others. In this human context of profiting from the accumulating knowledge and wisdom of others, of giving and receiving, of the strong caring for the weak and the weak learning to grow strong, the word "mongrelization" has little meaning or validity.

Q. 5. Would you want your sister to marry a Negro?
A. 5. It is natural to fear that a marriage between members of groups long separated will not work. Therefore, the question should be looked at quietly and honestly. Old prejudices will linger in many minds a long time after legal segregation disappears. Social barriers will crumble slowly. But here and there a young woman, a young man, will choose to marry into the other group. Such marriages "across lines" are taking place all over the world today. Japanese are marrying Americans; GIs are bringing home brides from the Pacific islands; Indians and Chinese are marrying Americans; Jews are marrying Christians; Protestants are marrying Catholics. For most who make such marriages there are difficulties.

If a girl asked my advice I would say this: the quality of the man you marry, his values, tastes, habits, health, ability to make a living, sense of humor, intelligence, his anxieties, his interests, are far more important to you than the color of his skin or the name of his religion. It is, above all else, important that you love him. If you are mature and have chosen a mature man, you can weather the storms that will come from crossing the barriers. You will lose old friends; you will be snubbed. But you will gain much too. You will find new friends; you can create out of your ordeal much that will increase understanding among people. What happens will depend on the courage and wisdom you and your husband possess. Remember this: it will not be easy to do; but it may be worth it. That is for you to decide.

Q. 6. Are mixed marriages fair to children?
A. 6. Children born of married parents will not suffer as much as children born of unmarried parents. There have been millions of children in the United States, millions in South Africa, in India, China, who have been rejected by their fathers and their communities because they were born out of wedlock and across racial or caste lines. These children have suffered intensely. A child needs a secure home and the love of both parents. If it has these primary needs fulfilled, it can meet hardships outside the home. But this we should remember: there is no need for a child of mixed parentage to have a difficult time. It is our responsibility to see to it that he is accepted simply as a child with a child's right to grow and belong to his community.

CHANGE AND THE LAW

Q. 7. Is not education better than legislation?
A. 7. Both are necessary. Neither will work alone. In a democracy they are mutually dependent. Laws do not *make* people good. They *protect* the people from those who try to harm them. Most of us can be taught to observe the rights of others, but there are the few who do not learn their lessons. The law is to protect us from these few and to remind us of our own obligations as citizens. No reasonable person would suggest that we not have traffic laws but instead "leave it to education." The word *education* is a bit ambiguous, too, for we can educate children to break traffic laws or observe them, to steal another's rights or to protect them. Which we do depends finally on our values, our sense of right and wrong. In a democracy we need not only laws and education but a clear moral sense of our obligations to others.

Q. 8. What right has the government to invade our homes and tell us we must socialize with each other?
A. 8. Our government has no right to invade our homes or meddle in our personal friendships. This is one reason for respecting our Constitution, our Bill of Rights, and our Supreme Court, which are three bulwarks against such invasion. Every American citizen has two kinds of rights: public and private. It is more often the citizen than the government that becomes confused about these

rights. When the Supreme Court ruled legal segregation unconstitutional it was protecting the *public rights* of a minority against a majority, in certain states, that had taken those rights away. It was in no way infringing on any citizen's private rights. There is nothing in the decision that affects anyone's home, friends, private clubs, or social affairs.

Q. 9. *Isn't the Supreme Court playing politics when it reverses itself? In 1896 in the Plessy decision the Court decided that "separate but equal" was constitutional. Now the Court rules that legal segregation contradicts the Constitution. Should it not be consistent?*

A. 9. Consistency is comfortable for those who do not like to change their minds. It is rarely a virtue, for it hardens quickly into the authority of "tradition."

The law is not an embalmed corpse: it is a living thing, changing as human conditions change, growing as man's conscience grows. The judges who made the Plessy decision probably made it, quite honestly, within the context of their times, basing it on the facts that were available in 1896. But we have gained a vast amount of knowledge since then. We know more about history, more about the human mind, more about children and their needs. World conditions have radically changed. Even words have acquired new meanings. For the nine judges who made the decision of May 17, 1954, to have sloughed off the knowledge and facts now available and to have returned to the ignorance of 1896 would have been shocking—and impossible. As Chief Justice Oliver Wendell Holmes said, "The life of the law has not been logic; it has been experience. The felt necessities of the time . . . have had a good deal more to do than the syllogism in determining the rules by which men should be governed."

"I have grown to see," wrote Justice Benjamin Cardozo, "that the [judicial] process in its highest reaches is not discovery but creation; and that the doubts and misgivings, the hopes and fears, are part of the travail of mind, the pangs of death and the pangs of birth, in which principles that have served their day expire, and new principles are born."

Q. 10. You can't legislate morality, can you? Look at the mess we made with Prohibition!

A. 10. To compare the Prohibition law with the Supreme Court's ruling that legal segregation is unconstitutional is a false analogy. A truer one would be to compare the decision with the repeal of the Prohibition act. Let us put it this way: Suppose, in the course of events, statutes had appeared on the lawbooks of certain states compelling minors and adults to drink in public places, and compelling stores and restaurants to sell liquor whether or not they wished to. Such legislation would have been protested on moral grounds by every decent person in America (including whisky manufacturers). Citizens would have appealed to the Supreme Court at once for a ruling on such laws and would have based their appeal on the premise that the United States Constitution does two things: it protects the people from *laws* that threaten their health or psychic growth and from *laws* that compel them to injure themselves or others. They would have won their case.

This did not happen. But it did happen that laws were set up in certain states compelling citizens to segregate other human beings. For many years this compulsory humiliation was not protested. But gradually the American conscience became more sensitive. We began to see the profound dangers of segregation, not only for the victim but for the entire community; we began to realize that we were being compelled by law to harm children; an appeal for a ruling was carried to the Supreme Court, and a decision was handed down that such statutes are unconstitutional.

Now let us return to the Prohibition act. There is a very real danger in alcohol, as we know. In recent years, we have begun to see clearly the physical and psychic risks of an excessive use of it by certain people. (But remember, we were not being compelled by law to use it.) The Prohibitionists saw the danger, too, but interpreted it as a danger *so great for everybody* that the government would be justified in prohibiting its use—as it is justified in prohibiting the use of poisons. After much urging, the sale of alcoholic beverages was banned throughout our country. This meant that no citizen could legally buy it even to drink in his own home. All were deprived, even the majority who can safely use it, for the sake of the few who are injured by its use. The law did not work, for it was an invasion of men's private rights—

as much so as would be the banning of sugar because diabetics cannot safely use it. A man has the right to make certain personal choices as to food, drink, friends, sports, even though to do so may endanger his health or his life. (To compel another to run risks is a different matter.)

Neither the abolition of Prohibition laws nor the abolition of segregation laws deprives any citizen of his Constitutional rights, public or private. On the contrary, rights are restored to those from whom once they were withdrawn.

GOD AND THE BIBLE

Q. 11. If God wanted the races to mix, why didn't He make us all the same color?
A. 11. I would like to reply to that by asking another question: If God had not wanted people of different colors to mate, why didn't He make it biologically impossible for them to do so?

Q. 12. Where in the Bible is there anything against segregation?
A. 12. There is a great deal in the Bible about concern for one's fellow men, the welfare of little children, the importance of the human being, love and charity and the abundant life, about the shunning Pharisees and the lowly publicans, about the Good Samaritan, about the brotherhood of man and the fatherhood of God. How can segregation fit in with these concepts?

ECONOMICS

Q. 13. Is not the race problem largely economic?
A. 13. Many who ask this question intend to suggest that were Negroes given adequate employment, housing, school buildings, and health facilities, they would be satisfied with segregation, and there would be no "problem." There would, of course, be numerous other problems which arise out of the fact that Negroes are human beings who have hopes and aspirations and needs and rights which material things can never satisfy.

Others intend by the question to suggest that it is only people who profit economically from race discrimination who keep prejudice alive. I prefer to put it this way: it is only people who profit in *some way* from race prejudice who keep it alive. These profiteers are of many kinds. The five major groups are the politicians; the mentally unstable who use "the Negro" as an object on which to pour their hate and anxieties; real-estate owners and businessmen who make money from city ghettos and "restricted areas"; a group of industrialists who use race prejudice to divide and weaken unions; and a few owners of large farms. As for the rest of us, we pay the heavy costs, economic and spiritual, of maintaining this system which profits so few and injures so many.

Q. 14. If you don't maintain restrictive (race and religion) covenants how can you keep real estate from depreciating?

A. *14.* It is prejudice that depreciates the price of real estate—not the fact that a Negro or Jewish family is living in a community.

From the long-range point of view the covenants probably aid in depreciation because they encourage prejudice. Perhaps we cannot remind ourselves too often that though we Americans have the right to live wherever we wish, we do not have the right to dictate who our neighbors will be. The problem of restrictive housing must be settled by establishing non-segregated housing as a principle of the American way of life. Non-segregated housing works. Prejudice disappears when neighbors know each other as people.

TIME

Q. *15. You can't do things overnight; it takes time; you'll only stir up trouble by pushing too fast, won't you?*
Q. *16. Is not gradualism the answer?*
A. *15; 16.* These questions are dead now. The Supreme Court has made its decision. We, as good citizens, must obey the law. The sooner we do so the more stable our community and country will be. The less we temporize, the easier it will be to accomplish the change-over in a harmonious manner. There is, however, need for preparation of the community. The time to begin this preparation is now. The place to begin is within one's own mind. Once we begin, numerous possibilities will open up. There are few Southern communities so bereft of leadership and resources that they cannot quickly and har-

moniously solve the problems which this change-over will present—if they want to. They will want to, once the people realize the harm segregation inflicts on all the children of the community. It is not a good thing for a white child to be given ideals which he can act out only by breaking the laws of his state. Either he cheapens the ideals (as most do) until he no longer believes in them, or he is in painful conflict with his conscience the rest of his life. This spiritual wounding of the white child, this disesteeming of our most precious beliefs, is part of the high price the white group has paid for legal segregation. That segregation harms the colored child is obvious. To be set apart, made "different," will injure the mind and emotions of any child. To be loved at home and accepted by one's community are necessities for growth; no child can mature as a healthy human being without this love and acceptance.

Once the community puts its attention on its children, action will follow quickly.

REASONING AFTER THE FACT

Q. 17. Negroes must be inferior—else why do they smell so bad? Look at their houses and the part of town they live in. Doesn't this prove that they do not value cleanliness?

Q. 18. What about their speech? Isn't that a sign that they are slow to learn?

Q. 19. If Negroes were not basically inferior, would they have let themselves become slaves?

A. *17; 18; 19*. These questions are so obviously unfair that one is inclined to ignore them; and yet they are used, even today, as arguments against giving up segregation.

Every honest person knows that poverty and hopelessness, ill health and anxiety, not skin color, cause uncleanliness and body odors; that it is poor schools or no schooling at all, not skin color, that perpetuate ignorance; that Negroes live in the poor part of town because laws, written or unwritten, compel them to live there; that their houses are broken-down and inadequate because discrimination in employment makes it impossible for them to afford better; that in rural sections of the South, ungrammatical speech is as common among white people as among colored people and is due not to mental inferiority in either group but to isolation and lack of educational advantages.

The important thing to remember is this: that in spite of the handicaps, many Negroes own beautiful homes; hundreds of thousands of individual Negroes possess as cultivated a mode of speech as one finds in this country; there are two hundred thousand college graduates who are Negro; there are women in the Negro race as sophisticated, as well traveled, as beautiful, and as exquisitely dressed as any women in the world. There are men of distinction, men who have achieved, men known across the earth for their intellectual and creative contributions to our world culture. This is common knowledge. It bears repeating.

As for Question 19, I list it here only to reveal the

depths to which a few people sink when defending the morally indefensible customs and laws which we group together under the word "segregation."

WHAT NEGROES LIKE

Q. 20. Don't you think Negroes like to stay separate?
A. 20. Yes, many do. Like all sensitive people, they prefer not to go where they may be snubbed or insulted. There are other reasons, too, for their tendency to withdraw. Compelled by law to stay out of certain parks, recreational centers, concert halls, schools attended by white people (and, by custom, out of white churches), they have had few opportunities to make friends across the barriers. Many do not have a desire to become acquainted with people who have put such a high premium on their whiteness; they doubt that they would like them. Such feelings are natural, even if a bit unfair to the majority of whites who are not arrogant, who do not overesteem their whiteness, who are usually friendly and decent. One can hardly blame Negroes for this unpleasant image they have of white people, for it has been built up (often unintentionally) day after day, in our white newspapers, in news story and editorial and letters to the press; by political speeches; by sudden, if infrequent, acts of racial violence; and by subtle acts of patronage. It is a distorted image, yes; but too few white Southerners have done much to dispel it. There is a real job to be done here, which each of us can help with.

Q. 21. Will they want to give up their churches and businesses?

A. 21. No. And there is no reason why they should. Negro ministers can compete rather easily in eloquence with white ministers; Negro choirs are as good as white choirs. Whites are more likely to attend Negro churches than Negroes are to attend white churches. The majority, white and colored, will stay where they are. The difference will be a freedom from tension which will be enjoyed by everybody.

The situation is likely to work out much the same way for business firms and professions: although the clientele will gradually become mixed, there is no reason why any efficient business or good professional man should lose his patrons. What will likely happen is that competition will raise standards on both sides of town. Negro doctors in several small Georgia towns have white patients. What people want is a good doctor, a good lawyer, a good teacher, a good social worker, and so forth. There are intelligent, talented people in the Negro race who have strong motivations for proving their worth. The net result will be good for the entire South. It has already been good for sports; it will be good for the teaching profession, good for medicine—for we so urgently need more and better trained doctors—good for the ministry, not only because each group of ministers will be challenged by the other but because for the first time in nearly a century an old burden will roll off the church's conscience. The great spiritual revival so many hope and pray for will come more easily when segregation no longer blocks the way.

COMMUNISM AND COLOR

Q. 22. *Why worry about what the Communists say? Look at how they lie about our lynchings. They'll keep on lying—no matter what we do.*

A. 22. Nothing we do about the elimination of segregation will convert the Communist party leaders in Russia and China. It will, however, give them a shaking up, for it will destroy their most powerful propaganda weapon: the use of *color*. They have used *color* as skillfully and as shrewdly as do our Southern demagogues, to arouse a billion and a half people's anxiety and hurt feelings—people not yet converted to communism. The Asians' and Africans' hurt memories center around "white colonialism." They think of democracy as "white democracy." They think of themselves as colored, and they make identification with every racial incident (small or large) which happens in our country. This is the psychological wall our foreign policy cannot climb over. There is a door in that wall. It will swing open when legal segregation is completely abolished in this country—a small price to pay for a good understanding with the free peoples of the world.

As for lynchings: it is true that one lynching serves the Communists and their fellow travelers for ten thousand speeches. It is not difficult to see why. A lynching is more than a killing: it is a symbol. Symbols are powerful in poetry or propaganda. They go deep down in the minds and imaginations of people. A lynching, in the old days, was cold-bloodedly planned and carried out by a group of men with the silent acquiescence of the community. Rarely were the lynchers punished. The affair was a kind of white-supremacy ritual, expressing profound and tangled feelings and threats. Any propaganda committee worth its salt would seize on such a powerful symbol and use it for all it is worth. It is worth far too much in Asia and Africa, today, because of white colonialism and the evils perpetrated in its name. Lynchings have now stopped. In the past two years we have had none. In the past ten years we have had hardly more than twenty. But one was too many. A colored man hanging from the limb of a tree is etched deep in the world's memory. It will require much good will and sacrifice on our part, and much forgiveness on the part of a billion and half colored people, to rub that image out.

Q. 23. *The Communists think segregation is wrong, and so do the liberals. Are not the liberals just following the Communist line?*

A. 23. Long ago, Jesus Christ worked for peace. Does this make Him, now, a Communist? He also worked for brotherhood and for the acceptance of all people as children of God. Does this, now, place Him as the First Communist? It is a strange and sad thing to see many people who call themselves "anti-Communists" credit communism with all the good, the creative and constructive beliefs and acts, which mankind has so laboriously achieved. Many of these good beliefs (and the acts that spring from them) are in every religion; some we have, in the past, believed to be Christianity's contribution to the human race. Now it seems we were wrong: these good feelings, these humane acts were hatched up (so the Red-baiters tell us) by the Politburo. It is as if these self-styled "anti-Communists" have no faith in democracy's philosophy about the worth of the human being, no love for freedom and human dignity, no regard for truth, no esteem for Christian feelings of forgiveness and mercy, no concern for the welfare of children (other than white children). We know whom they hate; we do not know whom they love. Perhaps they should tell the rest of America what it is they value and believe in.

YOUR USEFULNESS

Q. 24. Don't you think it does more harm than good to speak out against segregation? You'll lose your usefulness, won't you?

A. 24. Most of what we have achieved, as human beings, has come because we can speak. Words are powerful. They open minds, stretch imaginations, stir feelings. Words that give the green light to hate and anxiety can do harm. Words that awaken men's longing to be good, that stir their pride in the human race, their concern for the welfare of others, or that give new meaning to old events, can do good—if not today, perhaps tomorrow. Words that interpret events and acts bring intellectual order. The search for truth is one of man's two most powerful instruments of change; the other is love, concern, tenderness. But always there are people who do not want change. They will fight back. *They*, not truth, not love, will stir up the trouble.

As for usefulness: usefulness for what? To do right is a highly useful activity. To speak the truth is useful. To help rid the world of hate and fear and the old barriers which have caused so much pain and misery is surely a useful thing to do.

There was a time (it has almost passed now) when to speak out against segregation was hard. It was hard because in our childhoods we were taught *not* to speak out. We were taught this lesson as carefully as we were trained in our toilet habits. "Bad things would happen" to us, they said. And we believed them. Most of us were mute for a long time after these childhood lessons.

But those who spoke out found that not many bad things happened. One lost a few scare-easy friends. That hurt. People may say such friends are not worth caring for. Ah, but we do not care for our friends because they are worth it. We simply care; that is all. That kind of price was paid by those who spoke out in past years. (Today it is different.) There was loneliness—not because one was shunned; one was not shunned; the loneliness came from an inability to share one's beliefs and deep feelings with those who would understand. There were deep satisfactions, also: new friends were made; one felt in the world current; one felt "useful;" one forgot one's self now and then in the tragedy of others, in a deep concern for them. There were moments of exhilaration.

The melodramatic things? They didn't happen—at least, not often. Jobs? Yes, now and then one lost a job or was not offered one. But what does all this add up to? Not much. This is the small price one pays for engaging in an important and new and creative project.

It is a bit sad, in this great and amazing age we live in, to hear people carefully counting the costs, adding up the risks. Every day we breathe, we run risks. Why not run risks for something worth while? Why not stand up and be counted for something that has a little shine on it, a bit of the future in it?

There are people who belong to the future, and people who turn their backs on it. Each person makes the decision whether he will live in the age he was born in or keep catching at the apron strings of the past, whether he will hoard his "usefulness" or spend it trying to help create a world that will be better, more secure, and perhaps more interesting for more people.

SEPARATE BUT EQUAL

Q. 25. What is wrong about a "separate but equal" way of life?

A. 25. There would be nothing at all wrong with it if we were automobiles or refrigerators. It could be worked out with precision—all the machines kept separate and all given an equal chance to function, as machines. But we are human. We have feelings. We have memories. We hunger for esteem and acceptance and recognition as achingly as we hunger for food and drink and warmth. We talk, we dream, we think of the past, we plan for the future. We—two and a quarter billion of us—are human beings who depend on our relationships with one another and with our world for all we are and all we can be. When these ties are cut, we bleed.

Separate but equal are strange words when one thinks about them a little. We human beings cannot live separate from each other, if the separation is prolonged; and we can never be equal. *Separate* and *equal* are words that have relevance only for things, not for children. What we want for children is a good growing climate where each has the right to be different, and to relate himself to his world freely and fully; where he has tenderness and care, and esteem, and the opportunity to learn the meaning of being human; and where he can acquire the strength to accept the responsibilities that go along with his human status. Equality before the law, equality in the eyes of God, equal rights as citizens, equal opportunity to develop our potentialities are valid concepts. But men are not equal as individuals: they are different. We should not tolerate, we should treasure these differences for in them lie the seeds of new growth, new possibilities for the human race. Isolated permanently from his community, a human being can never develop fully and happily; nor can the community which isolates him. Each needs the other.

Books You May Want to Read

(THIS LIST WAS COMPILED BY PAULA SNELLING)

These books have to do with modern man and his world. Some of them are concerned with communism, others with the growth of nationalism in Asia and Africa. Many deal directly with race prejudice and its social, psychological, political, and economic repercussions. Only a few books are listed here, all of which are interesting and have validity for today's readers. There are numerous others of equal interest and importance.

AUTOBIOGRAPHY

Abrahams, Peter. *Tell Freedom*. New York: Knopf, 1954.
Buck, Pearl. *My Several Worlds*. New York: John Day, 1954.
Chaudhuri, Nirad. *Autobiography of an Unknown Indian*. New York: Macmillan, 1951.
DuBois, W. E. B. *Dusk at Dawn*. New York: Harcourt, Brace, 1940.
Johnson, James Weldon. *Along This Way*. New York: Viking, 1933.
Laye, Camara. *The Dark Child*. New York: Noonday Press, 1954.
Lumpkin, Katherine Du Pré. *The Making of a Southerner*. New York: Knopf, 1947.
Nehru, Jawaharlal. *Toward Freedom*. New York: John Day, 1941.
Smith, Lillian. *Killers of the Dream*. New York: Norton, 1949.
van der Post, Laurens. *Venture to the Interior*. New York: Morrow, 1951.
White, Walter. *A Man Called White*. New York: Viking, 1948.
Wright, Richard. *Black Boy*. New York: Harper, 1945.

FICTION

Baldwin, James. *Go Tell It on the Mountain.* New York: Knopf, 1953.
Buck, Pearl. *The Good Earth.* New York: John Day, 1931.
Ellison, Ralph. *The Invisible Man.* New York: Random House, 1953.
Faulkner, William. *Intruder in the Dust.* New York: Random House, 1949.
Godden, Rumer. *The River.* Boston: Little, Brown, 1946.
Gouzenko, Igor. *The Fall of a Titan.* New York: Harcourt, Brace, 1954.
Koestler, Arthur. *Darkness at Noon.* New York: Macmillan, 1941.
Malraux, André. *Man's Fate.* New York: Random House, 1934.
Mason, Philip. *Wild Sweet Witch.* New York: Harcourt, Brace, 1947.
Michener, James. *Sayonara.* New York: Random House, 1954.
———. *Tales of the South Pacific.* New York: Random House, 1947.
Narayan. R. K. *Swami and Friends and Bachelor of Arts.* Lansing: Michigan State College Press, 1954.
Paton, Alan. *Too Late the Phalarope.* New York: Scribners, 1953.
Smith, Lillian. *Strange Fruit.* New York: Reynal & Hitchcock, 1944.
Warren, Robert Penn. *All the King's Men.* New York: Harcourt, Brace, 1946.
Wright, Richard. *Native Son.* New York: Harper, 1940.

SEGREGATION AND HUMAN RIGHTS

Ashmore, Henry. *The Negro and the Schools.* Chapel Hill: University of North Carolina Press, 1954. A survey of how the "separate-but-equal" theory was being practiced in the South just prior to the May 17, 1954, decision.
Cash, W. J. *The Mind of the South.* New York: Knopf, 1941.
Dollard, John. *Caste and Class in a Southern Town.* New Haven: Yale University Press, 1937.
Frazier, Franklin. *The Negro Family in the United States.* Chicago: University of Chicago Press, 1939.
Halsey, Margaret. *Color Blind.* New York: Simon & Schuster, 1946.
Johnson, Charles S. *Patterns of Negro Segregation.* New York: Harper, 1943.
Key, V. O., Jr. *Southern Politics.* New York: Knopf, 1949.
LaFarge, John, S. J. *The Race Question and the Negro.* New York: Harcourt, Brace, 1942.

McWilliams, Carey. *Brothers under the Skin*. Boston: Little, Brown, 1951.

Murray, Pauli. *States' Laws on Race and Color*. Women's Division of Christian Service, The Methodist Church, 1951. A compilation of the laws on each state's books on these subjects.

Nichols, Lee. *Breakthrough on the Color Front*. New York: Random House, 1954. The great success story of integration in the U. S. armed services.

Powdermaker, Hortense. *After Freedom*. New York: Viking, 1939.
———. *Probing our Prejudices*. New York: Harper, 1944. A handbook for teachers; very useful for parents also.

Raper, Arthur, and Reid, Ira. *Sharecroppers All*. Chapel Hill: University of North Carolina Press, 1941.

Williams, Robin (editor). *Community Case Studies of Educational Integration*. Chapel Hill: University of North Carolina Press, 1954.

Higher Education for American Democracy. Washington: President's Commission on Higher Education, U. S. Government Printing Office, 1947.

Questions and Answers: The Schools and the Courts. Atlanta: Southern Regional Council, 1953. (The SRC will be helpful in supplying current information on this subject.)

Southern School News. Published by Southern Education Reporting Service, Box 6156 Acklen Station, Nashville, Tennessee. A monthly reporting service, giving objective summaries of what each Southern state is doing to implement or circumvent the May 17 decision. Available on written request to the Nashville address.

To Secure These Rights. Washington: President's Committee on Civil Rights, U. S. Government Printing Office, 1947.

Your Human Rights. The Universal Declaration of Human Rights. Proclaimed by the United Nations, December 10, 1948. Ellner Publications, 1950. (Obtainable at United Nations Book Store, New York.)

The Education Committee of the National Association for the Advancement of Colored People, New York, will supply information and aid to any community requesting help in working out the integration of schools.

ASIA AND AFRICA

Bourke-White, Margaret. *Halfway to Freedom.* New York: Simon & Schuster, 1949.

Bowles, Chester. *Ambassador's Report.* New York: Harper, 1954.

Buck, Pearl. *What America Means to Me.* New York: John Day, 1943.

Calpin, G. H. (editor). *The South African Way of Life.* New York: Columbia University Press, 1954.

Douglas, William O. *Strange Lands and Friendly People.* New York: Harper, 1951.

Fischer, Louis. *The Great Challenge.* New York: Duell, Sloane & Pearce, 1946.

Gandhi, Mahatma. *My Appeal to the British.* New York: John Day, 1942.

Hersey, John. *Hiroshima.* New York: Knopf, 1946.

Khaing, Mi Mi. *The Burmese Family.* London: Longmans, Green, 1947.

Lyon, Jean. *Just Half a World Away.* New York: Crowell, 1954.

Masani, M. R. *The Communist Party of India: A Short History.* London: Derek Verschoyle, 1954.

Michener, James. *Voice of Asia.* New York: Random House, 1951.

Moraes, Francis Robert. *Report on Mao's China.* New York: Macmillan, 1953.

Rau, Santha Rama. *This is India.* New York: Harper, 1954.

Redding, Saunders. *An American in India.* Indianapolis: Bobbs-Merrill, 1954.

Roosevelt, Eleanor. *India and the Awakening East.* New York: Harper, 1953.

St. John, Robert. *Through Malan's South Africa.* New York: Doubleday, 1954.

White, Theodore H., and Jacoby, Annalee. *Thunder out of China.* New York: William Sloane, 1946.

A FEW OTHER BOOKS CONCERNED WITH THE HUMAN BEING IN OUR MODERN WORLD

Barzun, Jacques. *Teacher in America.* Boston: Little, Brown, 1945.

Bennett, John C. *Christianity and Communism.* New York: Association Press, 1946.

Cassirer, Ernst. *An Essay on Man.* New Haven: Yale University Press, 1944.

Davies, A. Powell. *Man's Vast Future: A definition of democracy.* New York: Farrar, Straus, 1951.
Davis, Elmer. *But We Were Born Free.* Indianapolis: Bobbs-Merrill, 1954.
Dunbar, Flanders, M.D. *Mind and Body.* New York: Random House, 1947.
Erikson, Erik. *Childhood and Society.* New York: Norton, 1950.
Forman, Henry James, and Gammon, Roland. *Truth is One: The story of the world's greatest religions.* New York: Harper, 1954.
Huxley, Julian. *Evolution in Action.* New York: Harper, 1953.
Luthin, Reinhard H. *American Demagogues: The Twentieth Century.* Boston: Beacon Press, 1954.
May, Rollo. *Man's Search for Himself.* New York: Norton, 1953.
Menninger, Karl. *Man Against Himself.* New York: Harcourt, Brace, 1938.
———. *Love Against Hate.* New York: Harcourt, Brace, 1942.
Northrop, F. S. C. *The Meeting of East and West.* New York: Macmillan, 1947.
Oxnam, G. Bromley. *I Protest: My Experience with the House Committee on Un-American Activities.* New York: Harper, 1954.
Rorty, James, and Decter, Mosche. *McCarthy and the Communists.* Boston: Beacon Press, 1954.
Schweitzer: An Anthology. Compiled by Charles R. Joy. Boston: Beacon Press, 1954.
Smith, Lillian. *The Journey.* New York: World, 1954.
Stevenson, Adlai. *Call to Greatness.* New York: Harper, 1954.
Thomas, Norman. *The Test of Freedom.* New York: Norton, 1954.
Ward, Barbara. *Policy for the West.* New York: Norton, 1951.
———. *Faith and Freedom.* New York: Norton, 1954.

SCHOLARLY STUDIES WITH FULLER DOCUMENTATION

Allport, Gordon W. *The Nature of Prejudice.* Boston: Beacon Press, 1954.
Arendt, Hannah. *The Origins of Totalitarianism.* New York: Harcourt, Brace, 1951.
Freyre, Gilberto. *The Masters and the Slaves.* New York: Knopf, 1946.
Kallen, Horace. *The Education of Free Men.* New York: Farrar, Straus, 1949.
Lowenthal, Leo, and Guterman, Norbert. *Prophets of Deceit.* New York: Harper, 1949.
Montagu, Ashley. *Man's Most Dangerous Myth: The Fallacy of Race.* New York: Harper, 1952.

Myrdal, Gunnar. *An American Dilemma*. New York: Harper, 1944.
Rapaport, David. *Emotions and Memory*. International Universities Press, 1950.
Schilder, Paul. *The Image and Appearance of the Human Body*. International Universities Press, 1950. A book of great importance to twentieth-century thinking and tangentially related to the subjects under discussion here.